THE PLIGHT OF THE LESSER SAWYER'S CRICKET

Plays, Prose and Poems

By Curtis Zahn

Compiled by Clark Branson

With photographs by Gina Michel

Garland-Clarke Editions/Capra Press

Printed in the United States of America.

PRODUCED IN HARDCOVER AND SOFTCOVER.

Copyright © 1987 by Curtis Zahn
Photos copyright © 1987 by Gina Michel
Introduction copyright © 1987 by Clark Branson

The plays, stories and poetry herein are fiction. Any resemblance to persons living or dead is purely coincidental.

All Rights Reserved. Permission is hereby granted to literary reviewers to reproduce excerpts for reviews, and to teachers and students to reproduce portions for classwork. Otherwise, no part of this book may be reproduced or transmitted in any form or by any means, electronic or mechanical, including photocopying, recording, or by any information storage and retrieval system, without permission in writing from the publishers and the author. Ref. also, to the Notice to Producers, in the front material herein.

Published and produced in hardcover and softcover in 1987 by Garland Projects, Inc., Los Angeles; publishers of Garland-Clarke Editions/Capra Press.

        Garland Projects, Inc.   Office at:
        Post Office Box 5723   1610 N. Argyle Ave. #213
        Pasadena, Ca. 91107   Los Angeles, Ca. 90028

DISTRIBUTED BY CAPRA PRESS, SANTA BARBARA.
        Capra Press
        Post Office Box 2068
        Santa Barbara, Ca. 93120
        Telephone: (805) 966-4590

Cover and book design by Don Stepp.

Library of Congress Cataloging-in-Publication Data

        Bibliography: p.
        I. Title.
PS3576.A3P55 1987   818'.5409   85-73096
ISBN 0-88496-262-8
ISBN 0-88496-264-4 (pbk.)

TABLE OF CONTENTS

ACKNOWLEDGEMENTS iv

INTRODUCTION By Clark Branson vii

Three Plays . . . .
    Origin of the Species 1
    The Plight of the Lesser Sawyer's Cricket 33
    Conditioned Reflex 89

Stories . . . .
    The Absolutely Naked Truth About My Problem 127
    How to be Parallel 137

Poetry 153

APPENDIX:
A Curtis Zahn Resume (1956-1984) 187

ACKNOWLEDGEMENTS

Warm thanks go out to Jean Field for valuable conversation and other assistance in the preparation of this book, particularly the appendix portion; to Edward Ludlum and other theatre people, and to many editors and literary colleagues for their contributions to the earlier creative stages of the plays, stories, and poems appearing in this volume.

Conditioned Reflex, in a revised version, has appeared in First Stage Magazine (Purdue University); *The Absolutely Naked Truth About My Problem* was earlier published, in part, in England, and some of the poems in this volume have appeared variously in magazines and journals in this country and abroad. (Ref. to the *Curtis Zahn Resume* in the appendix of this volume.) All rights are the property of Curtis Zahn who may be contacted through the publisher.

NOTICE TO PRODUCERS

CAUTION: Professionals and amateurs are hereby informed that the plays *Origin of the Species, The Plight of the Lesser Sawyer's Cricket* and *Conditioned Reflex*, being fully protected under the copyright laws of the United States and all other countries of the world, are subject to royalty. Permission to reproduce, translate, film, stage, air or reprint these plays, herein contained, as well as the fiction and poetry herein contained, must be negotiated with the publisher and with Curtis Zahn, the author/playwright.
    Contact: Mr. Clark Branson
            Mr. Curtis Zahn
            c/o Garland Projects, Inc.
            Post Office Box 5723
            Pasadena, Ca. 91107

INTRODUCTION By Clark Branson

A volume of the dramatic writing of Curtis Zahn is overdue. The present book is small, relative to his sizeable output of excellent work over the past twenty-five years or so. (See the *Curtis Zahn Resume* in the Appendix regarding publication of his plays in periodicals and the many productions of his dramatic works.) Small though this compilation may be, I will vouch for it as a representative, good selection, and I think others will as well.

Valuably augmenting the three plays are some prose and poetry inclusions. The plays have been put to the forefront. This is partly due to the publisher's desire to put out a specifically dramatic book, but also because Curtis Zahn's plays have been considerably less represented in print than have his stories and poetry.

The drama/prose/poetry scope of this collection provides, of course, for a richer overview of the writer. For example, the Zahn dramas, in their more direct accessibility (and the direct accessibility of drama per se), lend assistance to the more difficult prose piece *How to be Parallel:* causing it to "stand up on the page" more. Similarly, the particular prose piece helps one to see more clearly what the dramas are ultimately about. When considered with the plays, *How to be Parallel,* a fairly typical Zahn experiment in the short story, becomes less an "avant-garde" exercise by virtue of its language affinity with the particular *verbal behavior* of his dramatic characters. The latter, as pertinent caricatures, are not very distant from real-life.

We can find ourselves in these characters. Or we find that our own day-to-day *loose talk* with one another is bedfellow to the verbally-schizoid Harry, Harriet, and Sandra of two of the plays and, to some extent, to the more grim personages of the therapist and patient in *Conditioned Reflex.*

An abstracted, self-absorbed *verbal behavior* is Curtis Zahn's subject as well as being the stylistic crux of his drama, prose, and many of his poems. His (tendingly soliloquized) word-craft moves into the saddle and usurps life itself: as he satirically mimicks what he observes of human behavior—and particularly what he hears (i.e., hears spoken, in and about). He tosses this word-craft back to the reader and audience as a disclosure of our widespread offense to the gift of life (for, in a way, we are what we utter).

Yet at the same time, we are more than our life-evasive behavior, verbal and otherwise. This is self-evident enough in his dramatic and prose works. Yet the greater body of his poems is what directly stresses this, in the poems' way of hotter, serious, first-person feeling for people, settings, and things (and animals as well): effectively underwriting the cold lampoonery of his prose portraits and, I should add, the comic cruelty of his dramatic caricatures (which are, of course, cruel in order to be kind on another level).

As for the vaguely Kafkaesque soliloquy *The Absolutely Naked Truth About My Problem,* it is a mainly simplistic parable-fantasy concerned with the classical totalitarian dynamic of self-estranged masses embracing a mass-personification or idol, in lieu of embracing authentic human community. (The main character's glib verbal exercise with "Faye" is like comic relief, yet is part of the same illness: namely estrangement.) In kind, *How to be Parallel* is a sort of Orwellian comedy-of-manners, American style. Most of the characters in the Zahn dramas playact in a similar way, in their decadent, talkative obliviousness to the concrete, or to common sense itself: common sense which, for us, lies right under their noses—like the burglar in *Origin of the Species,* who conducts his heist as easily as if he were alone in the New England house! Indeed, objects function as abnormally as do words, in Zahn's stories and plays, and it is interesting and amusing that the burglar is virtually the only character in the three plays who has a sensible relationship to the material and to the physical here and now. (Significantly perhaps, the burglar has no lines in the play, as if he were liberated from Verbal Behavior.) Joe, of *The Plight of the Lesser Sawyer's Cricket,* is another (though partial) exception to the Zahn mainstream: in serving as a common-sensical foil to the chaos that is Sandra. Yet he begins to succumb in the end (if thwartedly! on the telephone).

The Land of Zahn can be a rather grim setting at times. And yet the reader, and particularly the Zahn playgoer, are in for some unusual belly-laughs as well. I like to dub him a radical humanist-humorist; a moralist, and an erudite comic spirit who deserves to be prominent today—particularly for his more recent plays (completed or in-progress). For want of closer comparisons at the moment, I would characterize him with Kafka, Albee, Ionesco, Brecht, and the particular "Olympian" viewpoint of Shaw (that of sitting on high and observing with a critical sense of humor). Yet the outstanding *Lesser Sawyer's Cricket* piece is in a class by itself; a work of particular originality, I think.

Zahn's solution for human community is a big order, considering the terrible forces which work upon us. His contention—deeper than politics per se, or any *mass* prescription—is that things will not change very much until people themselves do. (Ref. to the "Marxist" waiter in *Lesser Sawyer's Cricket*.) This is an age-old dictum and valuation, and Curtis Zahn's left-of-center critique is, in the end, an appeal to individual self-awareness, and to the practical truth that people can change themselves if they want to. Social satire, taken to heart, is part of the work of self-awareness.

The fuller Zahn discourse, in terms of a single masterwork, awaits us in the play *The Escape, Purgation and Re-entry of Group N-17* (unpublished, and as yet unproduced). It is a Shaw-proportioned comedy of Americans and heavenly hosts alike foundering around in a strange rut immediately beyond the heavenly portal (sans pearly gates and sans Peter). Herewith, the Cosmic itself is a delimited function of its all-too-human American contemporaries. A philosopher once said, "As above, so below." Yet is it the reverse?!

A third generation Californian, Curtis Zahn makes his home in West Hollywood with actress Jean Field. He has maintained a serious interest in boats and boating, and is a painter and general artisan-craftsman (having beautifully designed at least two homes with his own hands). A dedicated pacifist, he has been active in the peace and civil rights movements and once served time under guard as a conscientious objector.

His fiction, poetry and playscripts have enjoyed publication in the United States, Canada, England, Mexico, France, Spain, Italy, West Germany, and Czechoslovakia—in editorial conjunction with Walter Lowenfels, Paul Goodman, Alan Swallow, Kathleen Koppel, Tom McGrath, James Boyer May, and others. His plays have been produced around the country and he has been a playwright-in-residence in theaters in several states. Most outstanding perhaps, has been his fruitful collaboration with Edward Ludlum and the Edward Ludlum Theater in Los Angeles, which saw the production of several plays; this in addition to extensive production via Actors Studio West, Pacifica Radio, the Pilot Theatre, and Theater-of-Note—all in the Los Angeles area.

For full particulars, including awards, see the *Curtis Zahn Resume* in the Appendix.

ORIGIN OF THE SPECIES

CHARACTERS:

Harriet
Harry
Burglar

THE TIME:

The Present

THE PLACE:

A Rustic Luxurious Cabin

ORIGIN OF THE SPECIES

AT RISE

Interior of a country house replete with vacation type things—golf clubs, fishing tackle, skis, guns, etc. A mounted horned animal's head is on the rear wall. On the coffee table in front of the couch are an "antique alarm clock" and assorted loose items, including a piccolo. Some drawers have been pulled out, things are lying around, but the general appearance might be merely that of a well lived-in, comfortable-careless hodge podge.

The burglar wears a stocking cap covering his entire head and face. He has been at work and smokes a cigarette through a mouth hole in the stocking. He is examining a silver cigarette case when voices are heard offstage. He will freeze and listen.

HARRIET: *(offstage, calling)*
Oh, Harrrrrrr-eeeeeee.

HARRY: *(further away)*
Yes, Harriet!

HARRIET: *(near window, demandingly)*
Harry!

HARRY: *(coming closer)*
You found the key?

HARRIET: Who needs a key? I just now remembered! I always forget that this window has no locks!

(Suddenly finding himself trapped, the burglar quickly ducks behind the sofa on which the couple will sit.)

HARRY: But Harriet! We can't climb up there —

HARRIET: Nonsense!

(Her face appears at the window. It is a rather attractive patrician face of forty years.)

HARRY: Harriet — Doctor Freeman warned me not to —

HARRIET: *(deftly climbing inside)*
Nonsense! You see how simple it is? I must have been a burglar in some previous incarnation!

ORIGIN OF THE SPECIES

(She turns toward window. Harry's face appears.)

        Now, hand me the wine. *(He does.)* And your attache case. *(He does.) (She sets them on the floor.)* And now — yourself!

(With a dexterous yank she draws Harry's arm through the window and we see a somewhat soft, corpulent but dignified business man who, evidently, has disobediently stayed away from diets and gyms. He is wheezing and perspiring from the effort. He gets one leg through but starts to fall back. Harriet gets a firmer grip and through heroic joint effort he comes through, but the momentum carries him to the floor. Harry rises, dusts self off, adjusts tie and buttons. Now he stands erect, seemingly confident, waiting.)

HARRY: Well!

HARRIET: *(expansively)* Well!

HARRY: *(glancing around)* Well, well!

HARRIET: You're probably thinking the place looks as though it were ransacked by thieves! I'm sorry. I should apologize. — but I shan't!

HARRY: Why, no Harriet, It has a kind of comfortable, lived-in look! My great-uncle's children are quite — carefree! *(pause)* You're sure no one's been here and —

HARRIET: Only my third ex-husband, that I know of — with that young thing from Vassar who's even more untidy than I. *(goes to him)* Uh, would you care to remove your coat and tie?

HARRY: Why, no thank you Harriet. I'm quite comfortable this way. — It's kind of a habit.

(He discovers the mounted animal head and starts around the couch toward it. This forces the burglar to crawl out to the side. He crouches there. Neither of them notice.)

        Moose! Is that the one shot by your first husband?

HARRIET: Elk. *Second* husband. The first was the skier.

(Harry starts back to the sofa. The burglar crawls in back of it again.)

HARRY: Yes.

(Sound of breaking glass. Harriet is unaware of it. Harry vaguely notices. He pauses beside her.)

Uh, Harriet — do you hear something like tinkling glass?

HARRIET: *Tinkling* glasses! Of course! You clever old fox! *(She jumps up, starts toward cabinet.)* You're reminding me I completely forgot to pour the Carbernet Au Revoir!

(Sound of burglar crawling in another direction. Harry listens but is uncertain that he heard.)

HARRY: Harriet, I — we — are you certain—?

HARRIET: Not a word, sir! Would you question a ripe fall afternoon of swaying trees and secret promises with some idiotic protest!

(She returns with two goblets, motions him to be seated again. Harry gallantly takes the bottle and tries to unscrew the cap. He cannot. With a dazzling coquettish smile she seizes it, opens it, hands it back. Harry starts to pour, then jerks back.)

HARRY: Spider!

HARRIET: Spider *web*. *(With Kleenex she wipes glass, hands it back. Harry hesitates.)*

HARRY: Uh, dust!

HARRIET: Of course! How careless of me! *(She wipes both glasses. Harry pours, but bottle rattles, and both glasses overflow.)*

HARRY: Somehow, I'm not myself today, Harriet — *(He gets out monogrammed handkerchief and proceeds to blot the table.)*

HARRIET: Why, how *could* you be!
Why *should* you be!

(In his nervousness Harry upsets one glass. Harriet helps him mop table, refills glass. They clink glasses. At the same time, sound of breaking glass is heard again. Harriet raises hers in a toast.)

ORIGIN OF THE SPECIES

                Well!

HARRY: Well!

HARRIET: To the forevering-after of tinkling glasses!

HARRY: *(aware of sounds in the room)* Harry — do you suppose —

HARRIET: . . . . And male and female
                Suddenly manacled to one another
                  By mysterious biological imperatives.
                    Stoned by the smoke of autumn's burning
                                          leaves . . .

(Harriet places long, ivory cigarette holder between lips. Searches the cluttered coffee table for the silver cigarette box but appears unconsious of the fact that it isn't there.)
                . . . . Oh! Whilst our world rants
                And silly businessmen go
                  About their silly business —
                  Harry and Harriet
                    Thrown down upon one another
                      Shall while away an afternoon and evening
                      Discovering life's intimate secrets!

(She tries to light the end of her holder, discovers there is no cigarette. Harry watches with increasing discomfort.)

HARRY: Harriet —

HARRIET: *(gets up, pacing, with long, seductive strides)*
           Yes? Yes?

HARRY: Harriet, I —

HARRIET: *(a curtain speech in swoops and postures)*
           I suppose you're wondering, Harry
                Why I've brought you here so suddenly
                    Of a pregnant afternoon . . . .
           (pause. She faces him before he would answer.)
           Is it the business of bonds or banks
                Or gold to be sold —
                    Or any of those things you do so well?

HARRY:	Why, I assumed — *(pause)* Why yes, of course!
HARRIET:	*No* Harry — not at all! Most emphatically no!
HARRY:	No.

HARRIET:	*(in a sweeping tour around back of couch without noticing burglar)*
	No! Nor has it to do with planes, or trains
	    Nor brains or grains—
	(She faces him directly).
	I've brought you here because you are, to me,
	    The Darwinian Man!
	Are there any questions so far —?

(She sits and smiles radiantly. Harry upsets his drink. The burglar stands up behind them and lights a cigarette. He crouches down again; rising smoke is visible.)

HARRY:	Uh — why no, Harriet. That is, I don't think so. *(a forced smile)* Yes! I believe I'm with you so far —
HARRIET:	Well, then! *(She smells the smoke. She rummages the coffee table searching.)* I seem to be mislaying everything! First my keys, and now the cigarette case.
HARRY:	Harriet! Do you smell smoke?

HARRIET:	Smoke? How could there be smoke when there's no — *(She breaks off and laughs gaily. Then sees that he appears worried.)*
	Are you sure you're all right, Harry?
	  I must apologize for the disarray of things.
	    I suspect one of my ex-husbands
	      Has rendezvoused with some gullible, younger,
	        Charming ladyfriend.

HARRY:	Why, not at all, Harriet! As you say, the place has a kind of lived-in look — what some of my young clients would call Good Vibes. *(pause)* Are you sure we're not interrupting something? Are you certain you don't smell smoke?

ORIGIN OF THE SPECIES

HARRIET: Of course not, my dear. Everything's been prearranged.

HARRY: *(pause)* Oh.

HARRIET: Now! Tell me truly! Does my proclamation come across clear and reasonable?

HARRY: *(confused)* What's that, Harriet?

HARRIET: *The Darwinian Man. (He stands up.)* I — don't go 'round calling everyone Darwinian Man, Harry —

HARRY: *(Nervous, he takes a few steps toward left stage.)*
Uh — we all have our private opinions, Harriet
And if you say that . . . to you . . .
I'm that which you say . . . well, certainly —

(He steps on bracelet on floor beside end of sofa. Picks it up.)

HARRIET: *(dismissive glance)* Bracelet.

HARRY: Bracelet.

HARRIET: Junk jewelry bracelet. Obviously
It belongs to one of Hans's junky lady friends.
(thoughtful pause)
Although, of course, it could be Harold's
Or Hank's.
Now! *(She gestures him back to divan. Harry becomes suddenly interested in the piccolo.)*

HARRY: Who plays the clarinet, Harriet?

HARRIET: *Piccolo.* Why no one that I'd know!
Would *you* play a piccolo?
Would *I*?
(pause)
Now! I'm talking survival of the fittest, Harry
And most men nowadays aren't fit to survive.
Not Nijinsky. Nor Stravinsky.
Nor Hercules or Socrates
To say nothing of Clark Gable
Nor Cain and Abel! *(pause)* Why?

ORIGIN OF THE SPECIES

(Harry has been fumbling nervously with the clock. The alarm suddenly goes off. Harriet is annoyed. Harry is embarrassed.)

HARRY: Antique clock!

HARRIET: *(dismissive, impatient) Reproduction. (pause)* Put it back on the hearth where you found it —

HARRY: *(confused)* But it was —

HARRIET: Thank you. Now! Let me go back for a moment.
(beseechingly)
Just a few million years — Visualize male and female
  Fused together under rollicking moons!
    As the lower animals stare
      In silent amazement!
(turns to him impassionedly)
Our ancestors, Harry!
  Fornicating desperately
    Experimenting assiduously
      In order to bring forth
        The prophesized super-race —
(triumphantly)
Us!

(The burglar chuckles. Harriet doesn't notice. Harry is vaguely aware.)

HARRY: *(uneasily)* Harriet —

HARRIET: Yes, dear?

HARRY: Do you have a feeling we're being watched?

HARRIET: *(peeved by his changing the subject)*
Watched? Who'd watch us?
  We've done nothing worth watching! *(pause)* Yet.
    (pause) Unless you're referring to Hans, Harry
    Or my most recent husband, Hank —

HARRY: No Harriet. I mean *Harold* — not Hans or Hank! Harold — the one who shot the moose.

ORIGIN OF THE SPECIES

HARRIET: Not moose — elk! Not Harold — Hank, Harry —

HARRY: *Hank?* Anyway, I get a feeling of Harold.

HARRIET: Again? Not again!

HARRY: Harold always giggled and I heard giggling.

HARRIET: Harold never giggled. *Chuckled!* That's quite a different thing — chuckling. Are you certain you heard giggling? We've done nothing to giggle about yet. Do I make it a practice to marry and divorce husbands who've nothing better to do than to laugh over dirty jokes!

(A noise is heard offstage. Harry leaps up.)

HARRY: There!

HARRIET: Where?

HARRY: I knew it was Harold! Harold always slammed doors. You told me so.

HARRIET: Nonsense! *Cat! (She goes to cabinet, brings out a cigar humidor.)*

HARRY: You've a cat, Harriet?

HARRIET: Of course not! *(She takes out a Havana cigar, lights it.)* Now! Where were we! Yes —!
   We were having a discussion
     Concerning male and female
       I found myself stating that you are
         Unequivocally
           The last Darwinian man —
(She blows smoke.)
This is not to assert that you're overly masculine — *(She draws on the cigar again.)*
Nor am *I!*
(She blows more smoke.)
As you will presently discover!

HARRY: *(nervously consults his watch)* Uh, Harriet — I promised Mrs. Claborn I would —

ORIGIN OF THE SPECIES

HARRIET: *(brusquely)* I'll phone my secretary to call her in a moment. Now! *May* I continue? *(She fluffs the cushions invitingly. Harry sits.)*
Harry, I've purposely avoided going into
   The erotic details
      Of titillating sex
         In order to bring about my climax. *(pause)*
Are there items which need clarification so far?

HARRY: Why, yes, Harriet. Do you have a telephone?

HARRIET: *Telephone!* Why, no! Why a telephone when no longer am I living here?

HARRY: But Harriet —

HARRIET: *(again searching for the cigarette case)*
I wonder if *Hank* took my cigarette case?
   Although it could have been Harold —
     Since it was a wedding present from —
(She pauses to remember.) Hans.
Harold never cared much for Hans —

HARRY: Harriet — do all of the men you marry have names that begin with "H"?

HARRIET: *(pause)* So far, yes! Have you any other questions?

HARRY: *(apologetically)* Yes. *(pause)* How can you call your secretary if there is no telephone?

HARRIET: *(absently)* Mmmmmm? *(pause)*
I couldn't call him anyway, dear
   He's somewhere in Africa
     Hunting Pigmies
       Or interviewing the natives
         In order to find out why their future
           Continues to lie in the past.

HARRY: I promised Mrs. Claborn —

HARRIET: *(leaps to her feet)*

ORIGIN OF THE SPECIES

>>I'm certain you did!
>>>And you're a man to keep a promise, Harry
>>>>Whenever it is in the least possible!
>>However —!
>>>A rather obvious situation is at hand —
>>>>Ourselves — Propelled here
>>>>>By some as yet undefined urgency!

(She examines wine bottle, pours remainder into Harry's goblet.)

>>And it is that which obtains. *(pause)*
>>>Are you certain I need not reiterate
>>>>The situation so far?

HARRY: Why, no, Harriet. — No. *(pause)* However —

(He reaches for attache case. Opens it, closes it. Now brightly:)

>>I'd need to have one of my secretaries
>>>Put such questions or ideas in order.
>>*(Reopens attache case. Pretends to read. Glances up.)* Miss Fairchild! She's gifted in these things. Understands my feelings. And reads between the lines.

HARRIET: *Good!* I mean that's bad!
>>I mean it's too bad men still use secretaries
>>>For such purposes.
>>*(She relights the cigar stub, clenching it in her teeth.)*
>>Incidentally — I'm not a member of that thing —
>>>That Movement —
>>>>Women's Lib! No!
>>Has it anything at all to do with the Darwinian Plan?

HARRY: *(As she stares hard at him, he obediently dredges up an answer.)* Why, no. I wouldn't think so, Harriet.

HARRIET: No! *(pause)* Now! Let us continue —
>We are aware, Harry, that Nature
>>In her assiduous search for perfection
>>>Eliminates certain species through default.
>>>>To wit: That enormous, invincible proponent
>>>>>Of *Massive Retaliation* —

ORIGIN OF THE SPECIES

(She gestures with palms up.)
Phhhhhtttttttt!

HARRY: What, Harriet?

HARRIET: *(irritated, imperative)*
The *dinosaur!* *(gestures again)* Phhhhhhttttt!

HARRY: *(obediently)* The dinosaur? Phhhhttttt?

HARRIET: Phhhhhhhhhhhhttttttttt! *Gone!*

HARRY: Gone!

HARRIET: And likewise the Dodo bird!
   It became so huge, so heavy
      It could no longer make itself — make itself —

HARRY: *(triumphantly)* Airborne!

HARRIET: *(pleased)* Phhhhhhhhhhhhhttttt!

HARRY: Phhhhhhhhhhhhhttttt!

HARRIET: There's a moral to all this, Henry — *(She stops.)* Why do I keep calling you Henry, Henry? — I mean *Harry* of course — now what I wonder, Henry — *(She stops, irritated with herself.)* There it is! *Again!* *(Pauses, hurries on.)*
What I wonder, is
   Perhaps you —
      With your adroit perception . . . . *(She waits.)*
Could kind of sum it all up . . . .

HARRY: Uh — *(He searches for the proper phrase. Finding it, will deliver the same with almost authoritarian confidence.)* It never pays to overdo!

HARRIET: Exactly! It never pays to overdo!
(now doubtfully) Or is it *under* do? *(pause)*
However — be that as it may —
   What I deeply admire and respect
    Is your infallible ability
      To tie it all together!

ORIGIN OF THE SPECIES

(pause. He is grateful, but also guarded against what she may say next.)

>When I come to you in need of a Truism
>>You're instantly there!
>>>Loaded! Well-aimed! Cocked!
>>>>No matter it should be a trite Truism,
>>>>>Should the purpose be served! *(pause)*
>Have you perhaps another apt cliché
>>Before I proceed?

HARRY: Ummmm — uh, why — *(pause. Now triumphantly:)*
Rather be small and shine than large and cast a shadow!

HARRIET: No.

HARRY: *(questioningly)* We all have our little faults?

HARRIET: Good! That was *exceptionally* trite — I mean, astute! *(pause)* Now! May I say something more about our past imperfect? *(Harry nods.)*
>I am told that as recently as yesterday
>>The American buffalo had no tomorrow. *(pause)*
>>>And in order to guarantee his future,
>>>>We re-examined the past. *(pause)*
>>>>>We've always been more concerned
>>>>>>With animals than people . . . .

HARRY: *(quickly, triumphantly)* To thine own self be true!

(Harriet shakes her head. He delivers the following with wounded doggedness.)

>*The meek shall inherit the earth!*

HARRIET: No, Harry —

HARRY: *(authoritatively)* The late Henry David Thoreau is said to have remarked —

HARRIET: *(waves him silent)* Not now! Please Harry! Not now! *(pause)*
>I've required your presence
>>In order to discuss the past

	As applied to our *future* . . . . *(pause; impassionedly)* And *we've not much time!*
HARRY:	*(Quickly seizing the moment, stands.)* Apropos of that, Harriet — I'm reminded I almost forgot —! I enrolled in a memory course this morning And it meets tonight!
HARRIET:	*(cutting in)* Tonight? Oh, dear! At what time?
HARRY:	*(uneasily)* The exact hour has slipped my mind — *(pause; now inspired:)* That's one of the reasons for *enrolling!* *(pause)* I do know that it's at an awkward time. Because I promised to squeeze in a few minutes With the president of Massachusetts Trust — Just before — Whereas *afterwards* A kin of the Mayor Is having another of those mandatory Receptions — for the Director — Of the Ethiopean Juggling Team. *(He stands, pauses.)* One might say that I have to —
HARRIET:	*(quickly)* Juggle your appointments?
HARRY:	*(frozen smile; then determinedly)* There is also a step-uncle The one in Farmdale, and, as a rule, On Wednesdays —

(Harriet waves for silence; a taut stance. An address to the ceiling:)

HARRIET:	Before me stands Harry Albertson! *(pause)* Please sit! *(He obliges.)* *Beside me sits* Harry Albertson! The third Though certainly there've been more Albertsons Than that! *(pause)* Indeed! Why — science could trace their ancestry Clear back into the trees and beyond . . . . *(brooding and mystical now)*

ORIGIN OF THE SPECIES

                Beyond . . . . ever so far beyond . . .
                To some erotic world of pond-scum biology
                Where he floated in verdant limbo.
                A precocious amoeba
                    Drifting in all directions
                        And vaguely determined to order
                        A New Order
                            For a disorderly world . . . .

HARRY: When you put it that way, Harriet
                I feel almost compelled to staying here
                    Instead of going there. Yet within an hour
                      The members of the Porcupine Bay Audubon Society
                      Will be expecting from me a few words
                        Concerning the curious nesting habits
                        Of the Lesser
                            Great Horned Owl.

(The burglar, having arisen from behind the sofa, is almost to the door. Harriet again places holder in her mouth and again realizes there is no cigarette. She places hand on back of sofa, holder delicately between her fingers.)

HARRIET: *(hurtfully)*
                Henry!
                While guns quarrel in the Far Eastern seas
                  And Irish immigrants scribble
                    Unthinkable messages on restroom walls —
                    And restless African cannibals
                      Invite Christians to drop in for dinner
                        And hungry Orientals pass empty rice bowls
                        From hand to hand —
                        Even as Doom's prophesied
                            By some ragged monk in Tibet —

(The burglar pauses, comes back to listen.)

HARRY: *(glances around)* Rome wasn't built in a day!

HARRIET: *(rudely ignoring this Truism)*
                Meanwhile, Harry sits —

>   Strong and erect! *(He impatiently stands.)*
>   Necktie firm!
>   Shirt and knuckles white!
>   His untouched wine cooling on the table!

(Resolutely he reaches for his glass.)

>   Harry Albertson survived!
>   A million million did not. *(pause)*
>   Ceasar is gone!
>   And Ghengis Khan
>   And Abraham Lincoln
>   And Dennis Shawn!
>   You've outlived them all, Henry. Why?

HARRY: Harriet —?

HARRIET: Yes, Harry?

HARRY: Harriet —
>   When you call me Henry instead of Harry
>   It is because you have some humiliating plan
>   In mind.

HARRIET: I plan the future!
>   There's something wrong with that?
>   The future grays; it's being taken over by us!
>   It grays like our cities, and, one day
>   Will become so dark we'll see the flash!
>   I propose to look it squarely in the eye
>   And I do! But I see only ourselves
>   Mirrored back . . . .

HARRY: *(authoritatively)* It's always a good idea to look ahead.

HARRIET: *(warningly now)* Excellent!
>   But I also glance behind —
>   In order to see what we're running away from!

(Harry rises, more at ease now. The burglar promptly dives behind the sofa.)

HARRY: It never hurt anyone to know and then glance back.

ORIGIN OF THE SPECIES

HARRIET: *(noting that Harry is about to apologize and leave; she quickly interjects)*
And you're *wise enough to know this!*
(Harry lingers, standing.)
That's what I so admire about you, Henry!
   You've that cold, analytical way of putting things
      Without ever seeming to intrude or show off!
You don't have to grope around
   For something clever!
      You just sum up all the parts
         Then *(She gestures.)*
           Make the whole!

(The burglar stifles another giggle. Harry is uncomfortable at Harriet's phrase, and also half certain that he heard the burglar.)

HARRY: Well I — *(pause)* Harriet! Did you just now hear a giggle?

HARRIET: A what?

HARRY: Giggle.

HARRIET: Oh! Like someone laughing at you? It's
   All in the mind, Harry. The unconscious sometimes
      Laughs at the conscious.
         It's a protective device . . . .
Now! Concerning your adroit way of putting things!
   Were I to say, "My left bosom itches— "
You'd come up with something comforting
   And reassuring —
Such as, "They'll *do* that sometimes."
   Or — "If it isn't the left one it's the right."

HARRY: Well, I —

HARRIET: *(cutting him off)*
Or, "The wife of the president of the Long Island
   Railroad
      Mentioned a similar complaint
         Just the other afternoon."

HARRY: Well I — I —

(He brings forth his pipe and glances at her. She nods. He lights it.)

    I *do* try to keep conversations on a constructive level,
     You see. There's not much kindness going 'round
      In the world today. People —
       Are overwhelmed
        By events beyond their time. And I —

HARRIET: *(cutting him off. Picks up the telephone.)*
    Henry! The phone's disconnected!
     Servants terminated 'till further notice.
      My last husband —
       And his future wife —
        Are shooting in Las Vegas.

(A door bangs upstairs.)

HARRY: Harriet! I hear doors slamming!

HARRIET: The wind, my darling! Always doors bang
     When the air's boisterous
      With pregnant promises
       And a moon soon
        Shall rise as though aroused!
    (A businesslike glance at him.)
    Is your equipment in working order, Henry?

HARRY: I believe it is. *(A sudden, anxious glance at her.)*
    However, Harriet —
     I've not had a chance to
      Check it out recently.
    (He seizes his briefcase and frantically opens it.)
    We've been extremely busy at the office
     Getting out the spring promotions
      For the Christmas season....
    (Rummaging around, he waves an advertising brochure at her.)
    Uh — Christmas, incidentally
     Is going to be pretty topical this year —
      I mean, *tropical.*

ORIGIN OF THE SPECIES

(She gets up, goes over to him.)

    Hawaiian shirts are back
     And a foreshortened version
      Of the old sarong.
    One of our clients
     Is fooling around with polo helmets
     And white linen suits —

(She pulls him to the seetee.)

    Everything repeats, you know —
     Ice cream freezers, for example!
    (He rummages for a report. He stands up to read. She stands.)
    Remember the kind your grandmother had —
     And you turned the crank
      And the cylinder spun 'round
       In salted brine
    Until, after a time, you couldn't crank anymore?
    (He looks at her imploringly.)

HARRIET: I never saw my grandmother.

HARRY: *(stopped)* I'm sorry. I —

HARRIET: She was struck by a golf ball
    Before my mother was born —

HARRY: *(confused)* Oh.

HARRIET: She died instantly.

HARRY: *That's life for you.*

HARRIET: *What?*

HARRY: *(awkwardly, gestures helplessly)* I guess that happens sometimes . . . .

(Her peevish expression demands an explanation.)

    I mean — being killed by a flying golf ball —
     I mean — it doesn't happen every day,
      My stepbrother was struck by a flying-fish

ORIGIN OF THE SPECIES

              Off Mandalay —
              And nearly lost an eye.

HARRIET: *(dangerously)* Henry!

(Burglar stands up again.)

HARRY: *(desperately)* Anyway, ice cream freezers are going
    To be a hot item
    This summer.

HARRIET: Why? *(She crosses to chair, sits. Burglar ducks again.)*

HARRY: *(shrugs, still floundering)*
You never *know!* *(pause)*
    Was she —
        Quite a golf fan?
        Your grandmother?

HARRIET: No. She was riding horseback at the time. *(pause)*
I guess it's pretty hard to tell
    Why some things are big
    And some things aren't —

HARRY: Yes, you never know.

HARRIET: No. You simply can't tell.

HARRY: *(helpfully)* Yes — It might be big. Then,
    Again,
        It might not.

HARRIET: I've got an old wind-up victrola in the attic.

HARRY: Why, that's marvelous.

HARRIET: You simply can't tell.
    It might become the ultimate in fashion!
    I think I'll play it cool.

HARRY: It's always a good idea to — *(breaks off)*

HARRIET: Yes?

HARRY: The president of Federal Consolidated

	was telling a bunch of us just the other night —
HARRIET:	Yes?
HARRY:	He who hesitates is lost.
HARRIET:	Yes! Yes!

HARRY:	On the other hand
	   It's usually wise
	      To look before you leap. (reflective pause)
	Seems to be kind of contradiction doesn't there?
	Was your grandmother fond of riding?

HARRIET:	(tone of impending irritation) Riding *horses*? (Shakes her head.)
HARRY:	Is the victrola in running order?
HARRIET:	(shaking her head; then, inspirationally:) Do you have a *screwdriver*?

(The question is not so unexpected that Harry instinctively feels in his pockets.)

	Please!
HARRY:	No — I'm sure I —
HARRIET:	Your briefcase! Look in your briefcase!
HARRY:	(instinctively starts to obey. Then reason takes over.) No, Harriet — I never —
HARRIET:	(thrusting it at him) Please! There's a little nut on the victrola And all you have to do is turn it—
HARRY:	(obediently opens the briefcase) Well I — (Harry's expression becomes strange as his hand encounters something inside. Harriet, seeing this, peers triumphantly.)
HARRIET:	*There!* What's that you've got your hand on?!
HARRY:	Why, nothing at all, Harriet. I —

(Harriet dives her hand inside the briefcase and brings forth an object. She

ORIGIN OF THE SPECIES

glances at him for an explanation.)
                Gopher trap.

HARRIET: *Gopher* trap?! But you live on the 23rd floor!

HARRY: It's for my Aunt Henrietta.

HARRIET: *Henrietta!* But she lives on the *44th* floor!

HARRY: *(gesturing hopelessly)* It's for Henrietta's gentleman friend! He lives in the suburbs. And he —
(reflective, confused pause)
    Doesn't own a bicycle!

HARRIET: Doesn't own a bicycle!
    Why not a *car!?*

HARRY: He *has* a car. *(She waits; he stands up.)*
    The police won't let him drive.

HARRIET: He's *that* old?

HARRY: *(shaking head, hopelessly)* That *young*.

HARRIET: Henry! What's all this to do with *gopher* traps?

HARRY: Harriet —

HARRIET: *(softer now)* All right.

HARRY: Harriet —
    Sometimes you manage — somehow —
      To make me totally confused.
    The gopher trap
    Is for the son.
      Of the gentleman I've been trying to tell you about.

HARRIET: *(consoled)*
    All right. *(pause)*
      Now! About the bicycle —

HARRY: The son never learned to ride one.
    The father's not allowed to drive a car. Alcohol.
    Aunt Henrietta asked me to select a gift —

ORIGIN OF THE SPECIES

    (pause) Birthday.

HARRIET: A gopher trap for her gentleman friend.
    It — Well —
     It's Freudian!
      In a kind of reverse way —

HARRY: No, Harriet.

HARRIET: *No,* Harry?

HARRY: It's for the *son. (She looks confused.)*
    For the *son's* birthday.

HARRIET: Oh. *(brightly)* Oh! That sounds very nice!
    Of Aunt Henrietta!

HARRY: As a matter of fact
    She's been *very* nice to him since the trial.

(He sees that an explanation is due.)

    Cocaine. *(pause)*
    I have offered to go and see him
     Next Visiting Day.

HARRIET: *(pleased. Charmingly:)*
    I would expect that of a person
     Such as you, Harry —

HARRY: Why, thank you . . . .
    As a matter of fact
     He likes to mount small animals . . . .
     And when I —

HARRIET: *(cutting in)* He *what?*

HARRY: *(gestures futilely)*
    Taxidermy.
     That's why the gopher trap. *(pause)*
    Harriet — I'm sure all this is boring you.
     Let's talk about your victrola.
      One of my ex-wives' brother-in-laws
       Had Edison

Singing on an old Caruso record . . . .
(pause)
Or was it the other way 'round?
Yes! It was Caruso sing . . . .

HARRIET: *(cutting him off)*
Apropos the victrola!
There's a beautiful young boy
At the Museum of Modern Art
Who's crazy about it —
The victrola! *(pause)*
He came a little after five one Wednesday
And suggested we go up into the attic
And turn on — *(pause)*
The victrola — *(pause)*
And since he carries upon his person at all times
A screwdriver —
I succumbed to his proposal.

(The burglar stands up, pointing a gun. Harry vaguely senses something is wrong.)

HARRY: *(disturbed)* That was very cooperative of you, Harriet.

HARRIET: *(noticing his agitation)* Why, what is the matter, Henry?

HARRY: Uh — I — was thinking about the War.

HARRIET: Oh! Which *one*? *(Harry shrugs.)*
Oh! That is nice —
I mean, how men think about the big things.
Like war. Or arithmetic!
Whereas women become emotionally hung-up
On little things
Like love.
Or screwdrivers. *(pause)*
Harry —?

(Burglar changes his mind. Now he tiptoes off stage.)

HARRY: Yes, Harriet?

ORIGIN OF THE SPECIES

HARRIET: What are you doing Sunday?

HARRY: Why, ordinarily, I stay home Sundays
　　　　And prepare myself for Monday. *(pause)*
Of late, however, my first wife's taken
　　　　To coming around . . . . *(glances at Harriet)*
We're still good friends.
　　And she has this emotional problem
　　　　With a young hosiery salesman
　　　　　　Who claims to have located
　　　　　　　　The lost continent of Atlantis.

HARRIET: He sounds quite re*mark*able!
　　You sound quite busy!

HARRY: *(nods absently)*
Unfortunately, he is involved
　　In some embarrassing way
　　　　With his teenage sister. *(pause)*
And she, incidentally, is the one
　　Who made so much trouble
　　　　For my second wife's oldest son.
I see them both Saturday mornings
　　Unless, of course,
　　　　It happens to be my week for mother.

HARRIET: Uh — *Saturday afternoon?*

HARRY: *(definite)* I work Saturday afternoon.

HARRIET: Late?

HARRY: *(apologetically)* No. *(pause)*
　　Around eight, I call out to
　　　　A little short-order place 'round the corner.
　　　　　　In that way, there's no waiting —
　　　　　　　　Though one could, of course,
　　　　　　　　　　Go over one's mathematical tabulations.
(brightly now)
But I do this during the soup.
　　And afterwards,

26

ORIGIN OF THE SPECIES

          During the long bus ride
          To the Asylum —

(Sound of a kitchen pot hitting the floor offstage.)

HARRIET: Yes? *(now suddenly caught up)*
          The *asylum?*

HARRY: Harriet —
          I don't like to belabor you with all these people.

HARRIET: *(impassioned)* But *do!*
          I mean — Hell, Henry — I mean, Hell, Harry —
          I'm enormously interested
          In your petty details!
          Why! Though one could observe that your problems
            Are *relative* — so to speak —
              Dr. Einstein's Theory of Relativity
              Bears a keen relationship
                To the Natural Selection
                Of Sir Charles Darwin!

HARRY: J. D. Ingram is not a relative. It so happens —

HARRIET: *(cuts him off)* That, alone, is remarkable!

HARRY: *(determinedly)* J. D. Ingram is vice president of the *firm.*
          (apologetic now)
            Though, of course,
              Temporarily on leave . . . .
          At least,
            We presume it to be temporary . . . .
              And, as a matter of fact,
                He's making a great recovery! Already,
                  They allow him to roam the grounds at will —
          Though, of course,
            The guards still accompany him
              On his little jaunts . . . .

HARRIET: You *are* busy, yet you seem so placid —
          So outwardly calm — That is —

ORIGIN OF THE SPECIES

HARRY: *(He is confused by this; but more importantly he wishes to establish a point. He delivers the following with unlikely power.)*
Yes, Harriet!
   Already, Mr. Ingram's missed the October deadline
     For Summer Casuals.
Things around the office are quite out of hand!
   What with Miss Robinson
     Still not quite recovered
        From a sky-diving accident —
And our chief illustrator —

HARRIET: *(cuts in)* And presumably you find time to see her —

HARRY: Five-thirty Wednesday mornings —
   If you mean Miss Robinson. *(pause)*
I also offered to look after her cat.
   Which, itself,
     Presents complications
Since it boards with an old man
   Determined to teach me Karate.

HARRIET: Harry!

HARRY: Yes, Harriet?

HARRIET: You seem to have a problem saying No.

HARRY: Yes.

HARRIET: However —
   You're not really a "yes" man —

HARRY: No.

HARRIET: It's something nobler than that.

HARRY: Why, thank you, Harriet —

HARRIET: And yet you are twice divorced.

HARRY: Yes.

HARRIET: Why?

ORIGIN OF THE SPECIES

HARRY: They *asked* for divorces.

HARRIET: And you were too polite to say No.

HARRY: Yes.

HARRIET: *(after a pause)* I think that was extremely kind of you.

HARRY: Do you mean that, Harriet?

HARRIET: No. *(pause)* I don't know.
    Good men are scarce in these times.
        And — when you do find one — he's busy.
(pause)
Originally, I had planned to give you my
    Love this afternoon at five o'clock, Harry.

HARRY: *(leaps up again, shocked)* Why — that's very thoughtful of you, Harriet!

HARRIET: Not at all! I'd prefer you think of it not as a favor! On the contrary — *(pause)*
    That is —
        Unless — *(pause)*
Are you involved with anyone at present, Harry?

HARRY: *(playing for time and knowing that she suspects that he is doing so)* Not really, of course —
(She beckons him to sit.) I'm still married to my third wife — And there are a couple of sets of children —

HARRIET: It is only natural that the Darwinian Man
    Would carry on the species
        At every possible opportunity!

HARRY: *(nods absently)* And there's a cousin in a senior citizens' home
    Who paints my portrait Monday nights . . . .

HARRIET: A large family tree
    Suggests a keen desire
        For self-perpetuation . . . .

ORIGIN OF THE SPECIES

HARRY: And of course there's a brother in Bermuda
    Who writes for money every Friday.
        And another sister
            Who's been an alcoholic
                Since marrying an electrician
                    Who practices weight-lifting . . . .

HARRIET: Problems, problems! Yet —
    They're alive,
        And carrying on!
        And that's what counts!

HARRY: Why that's a fine way of looking at it, Harriet!
    There's another aunt I visit Tuesdays —
        Who threatens suicide
        If I arrive late —
            Though, probably, she'll never get around
            To doing it —

HARRIET: Harry!
    I thought she was the one you visit
    Of a crisp, Thursday morning!

HARRY: Oh, no
    My stepfather —
        Ordinarily quite self-sufficient
        And, incidentally,
            A model railroad enthusiast —
            Suffered a freak accident
When his foot became lodged in a caboose.
    I go *there* Sundays.
        but at *three* —
Unless it seems feasible to remain overtime
Down at the Ward . . . .

HARRIET: Which seems a perfectly reasonable
    Thing to do.

HARRY: *(nods gratefully)* My *other* sister —
    Whom you seem to confuse with my other *aunt*
    Is the one in the *Ward* —

	The *other* Ward — She had herself committed voluntarily, which I cannot help but feel Was most courageous. *(He glances at his wrist and leaps up.)* Incidentally! You've just reminded me, Harriet I promised my Great Grandfather —
HARRIET:	*(cuts in; deep, dangerous voice)* What time is it, Harry?
HARRY:	*(sheepishly; glances at wrist again)* I — I seem to have forgotten my watch —
HARRIET:	I know.
HARRY:	*(in pleading anguish)* Harriet, my Great Grandfather Tripped over his violin —
HARRIET:	*(sardonic, but sweetly)* And you promised to drop everything And go out and buy him a gopher trap!
HARRY:	*(extemely agitated)* Yes! No! *(pause)* That is —

(The burglar appears in doorway. He is quite interested in their conversation again. He puts down the portable television he has stolen and leans back, listening.)

HARRIET:	Because you are chronically unable to say No!
HARRY:	Yes! *(pause)* No, Harriet! Actually —
HARRIET:	*(cutting in) Yes! (pause)* But not because you're weak, Harry!
HARRY:	I know. *(pause)* That's what John always says —
HARRIET:	It's because you are *good!* And *good men are hard to find these days* —
HARRY:	*(excited, pleased)* I know! That's exactly what *John* says!

ORIGIN OF THE SPECIES

HARRIET: *John!* Not the John Williams we both know?

HARRY: Why, yes, Harriet.

HARRIET: *(furious, agitated)* But he's — *(pause)* He's a notorious — *(pregnant pause)* Harry!

HARRY: Yes, Harriet.

(There is a loud noise in the doorway. The burglar stands there with stocking cap removed. He is grinning broadly.)

CURTAIN

THE PLIGHT OF THE LESSER SAWYER'S CRICKET

CHARACTERS:

Joe
Sandra
Waiter
Male, Female Voices

THE TIME:

The Present

THE PLACE:

A Health Restaurant & Deli

THE PLIGHT OF THE LESSER SAWYER'S CRICKET
AT RISE

The interior of a vegetarian/health restaurant & deli. A few unoccupied tables and chairs surrounded by too many potted plants at right stage. They face left stage and cannot be seen by audience. Most of the diners—"voices"— are there and throughout the performance cafe noises are constant—knives, forks, plates, conversation, cash register, etc. Also guitars, badly played, occasional singing, percussion instruments, harmonicas, etc.—a gathering place for a certain kind of in-group life style.

Joe is talking into a wall pay phone near his table. He continually turns to look over the unseen diners—obviously expecting someone to appear at any moment. He is dressed in a tailored Hong Kong suit, flowing tie, etc.— dressed-to-the-nines for an all-important occasion.

JOE: Thing is, she's already half an hour late and I'm beginning to wonder . . . *(pause)* What do you mean! *You're* the one who always says "Never Late on the First Date" if the girl's worthwhile . . . *(pause)* No . . . I thought since your girlfriend's sister brought her to the party you might *know* . . . *(pause)* The *Albergs'* party! . . . *(pause) What!* My God! This girl's stunning — you saw her! *(pause)* Come off it, Harold — you were drooling around her all evening!

(The waiter arrives. He is a young, blond muscle-boy and wears leiderhosen and sandals. He wears a tank top on which is stencilled "NO TAMALES BY GOLLY." He gestures to know if Joe is ready to order. Joe shakes head and continues talking. Waiter bounces away, flexing.)

The girl named *Sandra! (pause)* Snappy dresser! Chic! What a put-down! I'd say elegant! Patrician. Regal!

(Sandra enters. She appears furtive, undecided, perhaps resigned to the possibility that her date tired of waiting and left. She sees Joe at phone, his back to her; but he doesn't resemble the casually dressed man she met briefly while drinking at the party. She is hot, flushed, with hair uncombed and sans lipstick, dressed in wanton picketline getup. She carries three paper shopping bags and a placard which reads, "ABOLISH VIVISECTION." She stands, scanning dining room, at the same time waiting to see if the man telephoning is her date—if they will recognize each other. Now some-

one across the room catches her attention. She turns from looking at him and back to the telephoning man and cannot decide. Finally she slides into a chair facing the dining room, her back to Joe, and watches. A second thought causes her to prop up the sign so that it can be read.)

JOE: *(continuing, unaware of her)* Just like she stepped out of *New Yorker* magazine but in conservative taste — played down, and . . .

(He pivots again to scan the dining room, discovers Sandra with back to him. She doesn't seem to be anyone he knows, and yet . . . He turns back to the wall and continues.)

>Good lay! Is that all you think about? Is that all *I* think about! *(pause)* Oh, come off it! Naturally I have normal instincts, but this is different . . . *(pause)* I mean . . . There's a person there! One in a million.

(Something in Joe's unconscious causes Joe to pivot and peer at Sandra again. But he slowly, vaguely shakes his head and turns back.)

>Just because a girl bothers to dress nowadays doesn't mean she's on a manhunt! *(pause)* I don't *know* if she's blonde or brunette! *(pause)* All I know is . . .

(He pivots for third time, whips out glasses and studies girl but discovers nothing new. Puts them away and turns back.)

(He pivots again. This time he stretches cord as far as it will go toward girl. She senses this and waits. He whips out glasses, scrutinizes, but discovers nothing; puts glasses away and turns back.)

>*(pause)* Oh, *now* you remember her! *(pause)* Sure she'd had a few! That's why I'm wondering if she forgot. *(pause)* Waiting only thirty minutes . . . *(pause)* Of course I mind — This place is full of creeps!

(Sandra half turns, listening.)

>What was she doing at the Albergs'! *(Sandra turns now to face him.)* What were *you?* What was *I?*

(He turns again and they meet face to face, she with a shy, embarrassed

smile and a shrug.)

JOE: *(shocked, disappointed)* Excuse me, Harold! Something unbelievable just happened! I'll get back to you later! *(He hangs up. Addresses Sandra, concealing his let-down feeling.)* Well! It *is* Sandra, isn't it —?

SANDRA: I've no excuses! There are no excuses.

JOE: *(expecting an apology for her appearance)* You mean —

SANDRA: *(innocently)* For being late!

JOE: *(even more concerned than she, but trying to cover)* Oh. *(begrudgingly)* You *remembered.* Anyway —

SANDRA: Actually, I forgot! *(pause)* I mean, at the party I forgot about the march today.

JOE: March?

SANDRA: Vivisection! Unnecessary cruelty to animals. *(pause)* Why are you looking like that?

JOE: What?

SANDRA: Frowning! Upset —

JOE: Because I've no business being here at all!

SANDRA: Oh?

JOE: I was supposed to meet a client at eight-thirty.

SANDRA: *(concerned)* I didn't bring my watch. What time —

JOE: *(glancing at his watch)* Eight thirty-seven. Damn! I forgot all about it!

SANDRA: Isn't that amazing! Both of us forgot!

JOE: And there's no way I can reach him.

SANDRA: That was *my* problem! I tried to call you the day after the party, but — *(embarrassed)* I couldn't remember your name.

JOE: *(miffed, but partly relieved)* Warren. Joe Warren.

THE PLIGHT OF THE LESSER SAWYER'S CRICKET

SANDRA: No — the *first* name. It was something unusual — something unforgettable —

JOE: And you forgot. *(pause)* Ch*aun*cey.

SANDRA: Chauncey! Of course! I'm terrible about names. *(pause)* But it's not in the phone book that way —

JOE: No. I use my middle name — Joseph. Joe to the public.

SANDRA: Why?

JOE: M-m-m-m-m? Chauncey's too sissyfied. With a handicap like that —

SANDRA: But I think it's unique! Why should everybody be named Tom, Dick, or Harry! How can you remember if twenty people have the same name?

JOE: But you didn't remember Chauncey.

SANDRA: *(shy, embarrassed)* Seems like I didn't remember a lot of things that night.

JOE: Seems I didn't either —

SANDRA: Oh. About your appointment.

JOE: *(nodding)* That too.

SANDRA: What do you mean? *(She waits. He shakes his head dismissively.)* But at least we remembered each other.

VOICE: *(a man; calling from offstage in the deli)* Sandra! Hey!

SANDRA: Hi! *(She nods head as if to subtly indicate that this is as far as the greeting will go, and turns to Joe.)* It's one of the people I met at the sit-in last week. *(Joe nods, says nothing.)* He was telling us about his father who's a lieutenant colonel in the Air Force and yet believes we should stay out of Central America —

(She notices that Joe is absently wiping the silverware on his napkin and examining it for grit or grease. He realizes that she has noticed, although she promptly becomes busy with her menu.)

THE PLIGHT OF THE LESSER SAWYER'S CRICKET

JOE: It's not that I'm finickey or obsessed about germs — *(She glances up as though she doesn't know what he's talking about. He holds up knife and fork.) (pause)* Actually, it's because I'm *curious!* Does a health food restaurant really run a tight ship?

SANDRA: I'm curious too! Negative or positive?

JOE: *(examining napkin)* Both. Almost —

SANDRA: That's par for the course. *(pause)* Anyway, you have to leave.

JOE: *(examines watch)* Right. But there's still time for a snack — He's usually late for appointments anyway.

SANDRA: Good. *(humorously, indicating flatware:)* Are you going to eat with your fingers?

JOE: In a place like this? Sure! I'm starving! How about you?

SANDRA: *(nodding)* I didn't even have time for breakfast. *(pause)* But you seem so nervous. Perhaps — *(pause)* Why don't you just go on for your appointment —

JOE: No. The least I can do — *(pause)* I don't believe in breaking a date.

SANDRA: That's all right — I had to be here anyway. I —

JOE: *(relieved)* What?

SANDRA: I forgot about Henry. The *missle* protest. I told him we'd be here till ten or so. *(pause)* I suppose you're wondering what you've gotten into — the scene — me —

JOE: *(defensively)* I'm a square invading the wrong circle? No! In the first place I've always had a curiosity about health restaurants. In the second place —

SANDRA: *(brightly)* In the second place you may not be square. Innocent until proven guilty.

JOE: Guilty. But I could plead Nolo Contendre.

SANDRA: *(pleased)* Right! Which is what I, myself, pleaded when we were charged with disturbing the peace.

THE PLIGHT OF THE LESSER SAWYER'S CRICKET

JOE: *(disturbed again)* M-m-m-m-m?

SANDRA: The Evangaline Island demonstration. They were going to kill one thousand goats.

JOE: *(glances at his watch again)* Oh?

SANDRA: And all I did was go limp on the bridle path.

JOE: Limp? *(She notices his disapproval and adds, beseechingly:)*

SANDRA: Do I look as awful as your expression?

JOE: No! Of course not! *(pause)* But let's face it — At the Albergs' party —

SANDRA: I know. I don't blame you for being upset.

JOE: The fur coat — the long dress — that patrician look with the hairdo.

SANDRA: And you clumping around in Levis and cowboy boots.

JOE: *(sharing the humor)* I wasn't actually trying to fool anyone. *(pause)* You weren't fooled, were you?

SANDRA: Afraid not — though I didn't expect to see you in a tailored Hong Kong suit.

JOE: Tonight you dressed down and I dressed up! That suggests we —

SANDRA: Cared? But I always try to be well groomed. That's the woman's vocation! *(reaches down and pats satchel)* In fact I intended to become patrician the moment I got here. *(pause)* But of course there isn't time now —

JOE: *(indecisively)* Right. But that doesn't mean —

SANDRA: No, it doesn't.

JOE: No. You were totally unlike anyone in the place. I looked across the room — like the stories — the songs — *(pause)* I'll always remember that — that —

SANDRA: *What?*

THE PLIGHT OF THE LESSER SAWYER'S CRICKET

JOE: That night!

SANDRA: Oh.

JOE: You see — I'm leaving for Europe tomorrow.

SANDRA: Oh! My!

JOE: *(quickly)* And *you* were looking too!

SANDRA: I always seem to be looking — searching —

JOE: At the Albergs' everybody's looking — right?

SANDRA: *(shakes head)* I don't know. That was my first time — remember?

JOE: Right! That's why both of us took the chance! First offense!

SANDRA: But if you knew about those parties why were you there?

JOE: *(sheepishly)* Nolo contendre.

SANDRA: *(with a pleased shrug. She picks up menu.)* Since you're in a hurry we better order. *(Joe nods, puts on reading glasses. He reads, frowns, and then looks pained.)* *(determinedly cheerful:)* Shall I translate for you, Chauncey?

JOE: *(winces at the name)* An interpreter would be better.

SANDRA: *(understandingly)* Health restaurants seem peculiar at first. For instance, sauteed nasturtiums in papaya juice probably sound — *(She stops, realizing that he's covertly studying her.)* Why are you looking at me like that?

JOE: I didn't know I was. I didn't mean to stare —

SANDRA: But you aren't staring! You're judging! *(He slowly shakes his head.)* You think I look like some freak. *(He continues shaking his head.)* You wonder what we're doing here! You think I'm a mistake.

JOE: No! No, Sandra.

SANDRA: Well, maybe I am! Some people could say —

JOE: Did *I* say? How would *I* know?

THE PLIGHT OF THE LESSER SAWYER'S CRICKET

SANDRA: You wouldn't. You *couldn't* know!

JOE: *(angrily)* What brought on all this! *(She says nothing.)* I knew enough to invite you to Mario's Aegean Ristorante and —

SANDRA: That's all you remember? I told you why I couldn't go there! People who know better won't patronize Mario's. *(He waits.)* Too many taboos.

JOE: What?

SANDRA: *Taboos.* Things you're not supposed to eat.

JOE: *(looking around)* Oh! *Health!*

SANDRA: No. *(pause)* Well, partly that. The rest is moral.

JOE: *(as if not hearing)* I'm sorry?

SANDRA: Moral.

JOE: Moral?

SANDRA: Moral and/or humanitarian.

JOE: *(demandingly)* Humanitarian?

SANDRA: Inhumane methods of raising or catching the things on the menu. *(Joe glances at his watch.)* King crab for example. Did you know that the fishermen hack off the legs and toss the living body back into the sea to die? And Mario's special tuna delicacies! Know how many porpoises still get drowned in the nets? Thousands —

JOE: Excuse me! Where the hell do they hide the waiters around here?

SANDRA: I remember your mentioning Mario's Basque Lamb. You're not a vegetarian — but are you aware that the sheep-herders are poisoning coyotes? They're even shooting eagles!

JOE: *Eagles!* I've heard that's against the law!

SANDRA: *All* of it should be against the law! *(She reaches down, brings up one of the bags and starts rummaging through leaflets.)* This will tell it better than I can. *(pause, still searching)* Actually,

THE PLIGHT OF THE LESSER SAWYER'S CRICKET

most meat products are both — moral *and* health. The way cattle are injected and doctored up to . . . *(finds pamphlet)* Here it is! *(Joe accepts it with poorly veiled reluctance.)* The current issue — Ecological Health Bulletin.

WAITER: *(arriving)* Would either of you care to order something from the bar?

JOE: Sure. *(eyeing the tanktop shirt)* Incidentally, what's that all about?

WAITER: The shirt? I'm protesting the *Macho Taco* cafe chain. *(Joe and Sandra exchange glances; she shrugs.)* Dishwashers! They work under unsanitary conditions on account of the rich bastard that lives in Beverly Hills, Cal. that owns them won't install modern equipment.

SANDRA: But what good does it do to wear it here?

WAITER: It don't, unless I hand 'em a leaflet. *(He pulls one from under his belt, hands it to Sandra.)* Actually, I get four bucks an hour for picket duty there when I'm not working. *(pause)* They got mice, too.

JOE: In that case I'll have a double Scotch and Soda. How about you, Sandra?

SANDRA: It's a health bar.

JOE: Oh.

SANDRA: They make a good prune juice laced with marinated cabbage. *(to waiter)* I'll have that.

WAITER: And you, sir?

JOE: I guess a glass of tomato juice will do it.

WAITER: Tomato with shredded rutabager or the sunflower seeds?

JOE: Neither. Just tomato juice.

SANDRA: They don't have plain — not good for you. *(Joe looks from Sandra to the waiter.)* It's something about the acid content, you know — the way they grow them nowadays — *(to waiter)* Right—?

WAITER: *(shakes head)* I just started here tonight. *(pause)* I could ask Marge. *(pause)* Or maybe I could get 'em to make it plain, like —

JOE: Never mind. If it's all that much trouble —

WAITER: Thank you. Just the Prune Laminated then. *(He exits.)*

JOE: *(lays menu down, reads pamphlet)* Wait! This one's about Gay Liberation. *(starts to hand it back)*

SANDRA: Oh! Wrong pamphlet! *(starts rummaging through the packet)* You might as well keep that one anyway —

JOE: *(insulted)* What?!

SANDRA: *(scanning brochures)* Educational material . . . No offense intended . . .

JOE: How long have you been into this sort of thing, Sandra? At the party you were so — well, carefree —

SANDRA: That was a special occasion. *(pause, still searching)* I told you — I'd just broken off with Henry. You might say I was celebrating. *(pause)* So were you.

JOE: You were very charming! *Out*going — a little tipsy of course —

SANDRA: I know. I'm embarrassed. *(pause)* You tripped over the guitar player.

VOICE: *(a man; calling offstage)* Sandra Mavis!

SANDRA: *(holds up fingers to form an A-OK gesture, smiles, resumes sorting pamphlets. To Joe, offhand:)* That was whatsisname. *(still busy sorting)*

JOE: Who?

SANDRA: *(with a dismissive gesture)* I'll tell you later. *(She lays some items on the table, looks up. In a somber, pensive voice:)* Actually — Chauncey — I *wasn't* celebrating. It was a real

THE PLIGHT OF THE LESSER SAWYER'S CRICKET

                downer. That's why I was behaving that way with Malcolm — trying to forget.

JOE: Forget Henry.

SANDRA: No-no! The Whales —

JOE: What?

SANDRA: *Whales.* We lost the whales that day.

JOE: I'm sorry?

SANDRA: Four countries refused to sign the treaty. *(meditatively)* We're not much better off than six months ago. *(suddenly excited)* Here it is! *(hands Joe the pamphlet. He starts to hand the other back. Sandra shakes head.)* You can keep that one.

JOE: *(scanning)* This isn't about whales!

SANDRA: No, no — *Eagles.* I mean *porpoises!* You wanted to know about — about the — *(She cannot remember which.)*

JOE: *(ironic)* Roast Lamb?

WAITER: *(arrives, sets down her drink)* You cats ready to order yet? *(Joe reacts to the slang familiarity in an arched eyebrow way.)*

SANDRA: We haven't had time — *(smiles)* It's such a bountiful assortment. *(scans; pause)* Is the Brussels Steak medium or rare?

WAITER: *(shakes head)* I don't know — I've got this allergy to Brussel Sprouts.

SANDRA: *(to Joe)* You might like the roasted ears with loquat sauce.

JOE: *(straining forward to listen)* I'm sorry —

SANDRA: Roast cauliflower ears. You could substitute parsnip gravy if you don't like loquats.

WAITER: Sorry — that's off the menu, on account of the parsnip strike in Fresno.

SANDRA: Oh, that's right. I forgot —

WAITER: I could let you have grated turnip in papaya juice —

THE PLIGHT OF THE LESSER SAWYER'S CRICKET

JOE: Actually, I — *(desperately scans menu)* What about sauteed avocado chops? Broiled spinach —?

WAITER: *(shrugging)* Like I said, I —

SANDRA: *(waves to another person offstage)* Bill! How you doin'? Did you picket the Coke plant today? *(pause)* No. I wanted to but there was this demonstration outside the Vivisection Lab. I hear Ed and Mary went to work and got themselves arrested. *(pause)* Yeah. Talk to you later — *(to Joe)* That was Bill whatsisname! The physicist who dropped out.

WAITER: Frankly, sir, I can't recommend anything on account of I can't afford to eat here anyhow.

JOE: Obviously there's no meat or fish.

WAITER: Fish got a right to live same as anybody else.

SANDRA: *(to waiter)* Everybody knows that. *(to Joe)* If you'd rather have something more — more substantial — why not try the chicken-fried asparagus?

JOE: *(forced cheer)* All right. *(to waiter)* What goes with it?

WAITER: All entrees include a vegetable and salad.

JOE: They do? Think of that!

SANDRA: But some don't taste like vegetables at all! For instance they make a carrot dish that tastes exactly like Boston style clam chowder — cream style. *(pause, enthralled)* And eggplant waffles! You'd swear you were eating veal scallopini —

JOE: *(to waiter)* Sounds unbelievable! I'll have that — eggplant scaloppine —

WAITER: Boycott.

JOE: What?

WAITER: Cropdusting.

JOE: I'm sorry?

WAITER: They're cropdusting all over the place.

THE PLIGHT OF THE LESSER SAWYER'S CRICKET

JOE: What place?

SANDRA: He means where the eggplant comes from.

JOE: But they wash it off don't they for God's sake?

SANDRA: Sure!

WAITER: Natch!

SANDRA: It's not the eggplant — it's the birds! Did you know that by actual count seventeen crows, three owls, and thirty-two bush-tits — *(sees that Joe is startled by the word)* — birds! — were found to be laying soft-shelled eggs after the last spraying?! To say nothing of wood rats! Snakes! Gophers — even tadpoles. *(noting Joe's confusion)* Tadpoles are the same as your ordinary pollywogs.

WAITER: And if you got no frogs you got a unbalanced ecology.

SANDRA: *(discovers someone waving to her, returns greeting)* Hi, Henry. *(to Joe)* It's Henry.

JOE: *(peering)* Which one?

SANDRA: *(calling)* Imagine meeting you here! *(to Joe, lowered voice)* The one standing next to that elderly woman.

JOE: There are two men. One's bald, and —

SANDRA: *(cutting in)* Not bald! Henry had his head shaved in protest.

WAITER: *(eagerly looking)* You mean because of the coyote traps? Wow!

SANDRA: No, no! Ocean drilling! *(to Joe)* You see, Henry's into pollution.

WAITER: I was all set to do that myself but my girlfriend said No Way! Even though we got oil all over ourselves at the beach and there was dead fish who stunk like . . . *(pause)* . . . *(to Joe)* She was blonde and six foot two. Imagine!

JOE: *(polite, sympathetic)* You don't see her anymore —

WAITER: Not since yesterday I don't! And after she brought me these genuine leather leiderhosen and everything.

THE PLIGHT OF THE LESSER SAWYER'S CRICKET

SANDRA: *(glancing at them)* Leather! How come! Vegetarians are not supposed to —

WAITER: I am not now nor have I ever been a vegetarian.

JOE: How's that?

SANDRA: What? Then how come they let you work here?

WAITER: *Because.*

JOE: Because what?

WAITER: Because they can't afford to hire a regular waiter. I'm a body builder by profession. *(pause)* However — so far it's like being an actor — you got to have a job.

SANDRA: *(politely)* What did you do before coming here — before yesterday?

WAITER: Plumber. Only I quit on account of plastic pipe.

JOE: *(trying to feign interest. Now something in the deli section offstage gets his attention.)* Sandra! What's that man doing up on the counter?

SANDRA: *(looks; dismisses)* Excercises.

WAITER: *(squints)* Pushups. *(marvelling)* And he's thirty-seven years old!

JOE: But why does he have to do it here?

WAITER: You got to keep *fit!*

SANDRA: So what's wrong with it? Nobody's paying the least attention.

JOE: I noticed.

WAITER: *(enthusiastically to Sandra)* There was another guy earlier who does cartwheels! Eats nothing but mature fruit.

SANDRA: *(knowledgeable nod)* Only ripe fruit picked up after it falls.

WAITER: *(more knowledgeable, correcting her)* Falls *voluntarily!* (She nods, obliging agreement. This he mistakes as rapport. He adds:)* Same thing as the Nutitarian philosophy. Right?

SANDRA: *(he's wrong)* Well — *(pause)* Except that the Nutitarians won't eat fruit! *(to Joe)* But you don't want to hear about all this —

JOE: I *do* want to hear about plastic pipe! According to —

SANDRA: *(worried)* Shouldn't you be watching the time?

JOE: Yeah. *(to waiter)* According to the D.A.A.L. certain liquids passing through it can cause skin rashes, and —

WAITER: *(cuts him off)* Diahrea and puking! *(Joe winces.)* But that isn't my reason for quitting! *(pause)* Exploitation of the underdog! Inhuman safety precautions! You got plastic pipe on account if it's an entire capitalistic plot! Screw the common man! Fuck health — *(quickly to Sandra)* Excuse me, lady —

SANDRA: *(wholly unperterbed by the profanity)* M-m-m-m-m? *(Her attention is caught by someone offstage.)*

WAITER: I didn't mean to say "fuck."

SANDRA: *(nods absently)* There's some girl in the deli who seems to be trying to get your attention.

WAITER: *(following Sandra's gaze. Hurriedly now:)* It's Marge. You people ready to order — on account of she's giving me queer looks.

JOE: In a minute. I want to know why you don't just use *copper* pipe.

SANDRA: *(astonished)* Copper?!

WAITER: Copper sucks! *(Joe glances confusedly from one to the other.)*

SANDRA: You haven't heard about it? *(starts to rummage through pamphlets)* — I have it right here!

WAITER: *(to Joe)* You're asking me to whore just to make a buck, my friend?

JOE: *(forcefully)* I never suggested any such —

WAITER: Cartels! South America! The C.I.A.! Dictators!

SANDRA: *(rummaging)* Air Pollution! Contaminated rivers! Acid rain!

THE PLIGHT OF THE LESSER SAWYER'S CRICKET

(pause) It's even mentioned in *Ozone Digest!*

JOE: I didn't see anything in *Newsweek.*

WAITER: Natch. The fascist press never —

JOE: *(peering toward deli section)* Hold it! Your lady friend is signalling again —

WAITER: Thanks, I — *(waves to her and starts to go)*

SANDRA: Wait! Ask her how is it they're allowed to serve Eggs Montebello? *Samaritan Journal* has it on the shit — *(pause)* hit — list.

WAITER: *(stops, shakes head)* Marge just started work too! Actually she's in training for the 400 meter Olympic Relays Team. She doesn't know anything about —

SANDRA: *(cuts him off)* Whoever then! Don't they know there's a boycott on eggs and chickens?! *(to Joe, impassioned)* All baby roosters are put to sleep!

JOE: Put to sleep?

SANDRA: Gassed! The moment they're born!

WAITER: *(having hurried back; excitedly:)* It's true! My girl told me! *Holocaust!*

JOE: You mean to say —

WAITER: The Armageddon!

SANDRA: Mass slaughter! Just because —

WAITER: *(cutting in)* Just because it so happens roosters never learned to lay eggs! *(pause)* Exploitation! Genocide! Same old capitalistic system! If they can't squeeze a profit out of your own sweat and blood — *(gestures having throat slashed, with appropriate gurgling)*

(Sandra and Joe have noticed that Marge is still signalling frantically. The waiter, following their gaze, sees and starts off again.)

I'll — excuse — okay Marge —

THE PLIGHT OF THE LESSER SAWYER'S CRICKET

SANDRA: *(calling)* Tell the manager that everything on the menu is questionable. I'm not coming back.

JOE: *(calling)* Meanwhile, just bring me a bowl of alfalfa boullion as fast as possible.

WAITER: *(turns, gestures)* That should be crossed out! Chicano strike.

JOE: *(exasperated)* Anything then! Just bring me anything you have that isn't screwed up!

WAITER: Arabian noodles with dehydrated cherry nectar? Okay? *(He hurries away.) (A moment of armed repose while we hear a harmoinca struggling with "We Shall Overcome" above restaurant noise.)*

JOE: Look, Sandra. If everything upsets you so, why do you come here?

SANDRA: I've never been here before in my life!

JOE: *What?*

SANDRA: Henry's sister's boyfriend recommended it. I should have known better. *(Joe waits. She once again becomes endearing.)* — I didn't mean to become emotional.

JOE: But you *are* emotional. Right? And that waiter —

SANDRA: There is no excuse for public display. I lost control —

JOE: Well — that's one of the things about Women's Lib. I happen —

SANDRA: Women's Liberation! I want nothing to do with things like that!

JOE: *(totally surprised)* You don't?

SANDRA: I think it's self-indulgent! Narcissistic! It's all a noisy teapot tempest! I — I — *(She busily shuffles the leaflets; glances up to see that Joe is waiting for an explanation.)* I'll explain later. *(finds brochure)* Here it *is!* Plastic pipes!

JOE: *(still lost on Lib)* What? *(She hands it to him. He reads,*

THE PLIGHT OF THE LESSER SAWYER'S CRICKET

frowns.)

SANDRA: Wait! Wrong again! That's *Asbestos Poisoning,* isn't it? *(Joe nods confusedly.)* Isn't that funny! I had it right here — *(She wildly thumbs papers again, then tosses the entire packet onto the table.)* Oh, never mind! You ought to read that one anyway.

JOE: *(absently; he is reading)* M-m-m-m-m-m?

SANDRA: *Asbestos.*

JOE: I know. I'm trying to.

SANDRA: I didn't mean *now.* I feel I should explain something first. Do you have time? *(Joe nods.)* About my getting worked up and embarrassing you —

JOE: *Me* embarrassed!? *No way!*

SANDRA: Well, *I'm* embarrassed!

JOE: But not me! Just because some girl on a date blows her cover and — *(pause)* You assume that because other guys get uptight and scared — Also I have to —

SANDRA: No! I just want to explain why I'm unusually upset! I never told you why — *(She stops; he waits.)* It's because I'm having a hard time raising bail.

JOE: *(He upsets glass, tries to grab it; his fork clatters to the floor.)* You said —?

SANDRA: *Bail.* For the Salazar Lab demonstration in March *(pause)* I was one of the ones who scaled the wall and got arrested.

JOE: Oh. What were they trying to demonstrate?

SANDRA: *We* were demonstrating. Anti-missile cone. *(brightly)* Maybe you saw me on TV and didn't know it!

JOE: *(shaking head)* I don't watch TV. Only the ball game —

SANDRA: It was in the papers too.

JOE: I don't have much time to read nowadays. *(pause)* How is it you can be here if you can't raise bail?

THE PLIGHT OF THE LESSER SAWYER'S CRICKET

SANDRA: They just book and release you on your own recognizance. But if you're sentenced at the trials you have to have bail money or get locked up. *(pause)* Incidentally, when the waiter comes back ask him if the Grapefruit Souffle contains dairy products — I don't want to start another scene.

JOE: Are all dairy products — *(pause)* Are they all in trouble?

SANDRA: All except yogurt at the moment.

JOE: Yogurt. I can't stand it!

SANDRA: Neither can I! The kids eat it frozen because it's featured on TV. *(pause, concerned)* Chauncey — I'm concerned. If the waiter doesn't hurry you won't have time to —

JOE: *(glances at watch)* What's the diff? I'm already late.

SANDRA: *(sincerely)* I'm afraid part of it's my fault —

VOICE: *(a girl; calling)* Sandy! Hi! How do you like the coat?!

SANDRA: Hi! Looks better on you than me! *(to Joe)* Friend of mine —

JOE: It looks a little out of place in here doesn't it? Like the one *you* were wearing at the —

SANDRA: It is. I sold it to her —

JOE: The coat? Why?

SANDRA: *(nodding)* And my TV set. *(He waits.)* Bail money.

JOE: *(upset)* That beautiful mink coat!

SANDRA: *Mink!?* It's *synthetic. I* couldn't wear some animal's skin, Chauncey! — Same with the leather trim — Plastic.

JOE: *(a shrug)* Whatever. On you it looked like Saks Fifth Avenue.

SANDRA: I couldn't afford a fur coat even if I had no morals.

JOE: Morals? *(pause)* — But that long, brocade dress.

SANDRA: Thrift shop.

JOE: *(at a loss)* Interesting!

53

THE PLIGHT OF THE LESSER SAWYER'S CRICKET

SANDRA: Mmm.

JOE: And yet you're head of your department at work. Surely —

SANDRA: Was.

JOE: Fired? *(pause)* Because of — the arrest?

SANDRA: No. Quit. *(He waits.)* I resigned because of the Sawyer's cricket.

JOE: You — *(pause)*

SANDRA: *Lesser Sawyer's cricket!* My company is involved — *(pause)* Indirectly, of course — *(She picks up a glass of water, examines it critically, tastes it. Frowns.)* Chlorinated. *(pause)* Maybe I was a little hasty. Actually, we're supplying the blueprints for the engineering research. *(gestures)* I *could* have waited until they decide — then quit in protest —

JOE: I don't think I —

SANDRA: The Hooton dam! *(She sees he is baffled. Hurries on.)* They want to build the dam on the breeding grounds.

WAITER: *(with elaborate tray of food)* Sorry it took so long.

JOE: *(aghast)* I didn't order all that, did I?

SANDRA: *(inspecting approvingly)* Goes with the boullion — The hors d'oeuvres Cornucopia! Lichee nuts — ice plant — wild hibiscus stems — crushed geranium petals — cactus pears — pinions in shell — sumac seeds — marigold berries — my!

WAITER: No sumac seeds — *(dismissively; starts to leave)* Fire Department law —

JOE: *(to Sandra)* How's that?

WAITER: Fire Department. They make you cut down sumac bushes this time of year. Safety hazzard. *(exits)*

SANDRA: The Indians practically lived on them — *(She sees Joe preoccupied; waits.)*

JOE: *(not interested. He is wondering if she dated him to borrow money.)* They did? *(pause)* So you're temporarily short on

THE PLIGHT OF THE LESSER SAWYER'S CRICKET

funds —

SANDRA: No. *(pause)* Yes. I'm always short — There are so many worthwhile organizations that want contributions. *(laughter)* As soon as you help one, a dozen others send pleading letters.

JOE: So what happens? If you can't pay the fine you have a jail sentence on your record.

SANDRA: Too late! I already have half a dozen.

JOE: Really? *(He pushes hors d'oeuvres tray aside with a frown.)* All for worthwhile causes, crickets, or —

SANDRA: Not all. One was for — well, drugs. Another was for something just as silly — defacing the entrance of the Guggenheim Museum. Artists Protest demonstration—

JOE: You paint?

SANDRA: *(shakes head)* Just trendy at the time. My father bailed me out. He was deeply wounded and I — *(She sees that Joe has disgustedly shoved his plate aside. She samples some of the hors d'oeuvres and frowns.)* I see why you're not eating. *(Shakes head, makes a face but continues picking out morsels.)*

JOE: I'm glad somebody feels the same way! But why are you?

SANDRA: I have to.

JOE: What?

SANDRA: *Moral.* It's cruel and inhumane to waste food when millions are starving.

JOE: Jesus!

SANDRA: Any food. The tiniest, rancid, rotting scrap! India and the destitute countries! I was with the Peace Corps until I couldn't stand it any longer. Babies, old people, walking skeletons — *(Unconsciously, she starts eating faster and faster.)* Their withered hands outstretched — vacant eyes no longer able to plead — *(She notices that Joe has bent over and is intently scrutinizing the floor.)* What are you looking at?

THE PLIGHT OF THE LESSER SAWYER'S CRICKET

JOE: Ants.

SANDRA: Oh. Anyway — enough about wasting food. My point is — *(She observes that Joe is concerned that the ants might crawl on him.)* Is something wrong?

JOE: *(bravado)* Oh, no — I was just wondering where they are coming from.

SANDRA: *(indicating other table)* Why, over there — probably some spilled food. *(pause)* Uh, Chauncey — what was it you were asking before I got off on a tangent? *(She continues eating morsels and will do so until platter is empty.)*

JOE: About your father. How come he doesn't bail you out now?

SANDRA: *(smiles)* He hasn't been invited. I didn't want him to know about it the other time but he recognized me on TV.

JOE: *(admires her for this; feels safer)* I got into trouble once. Neighbor's plate glass window. But nobody came to my rescue. The old man was an unemployed security guard with five kids and no wife.

WAITER: *(arriving, carries a thick book)* Here I am again! Ready to order yet?

SANDRA: *(polite but firm)* Ready *not* to order! The hors d'oeuvres are borderline. They're supposed to be crisp! Fresh! Chilled! I have a suspicion they're not even organically grown. And the eucalyptus-oil dressing —

WAITER: I know! Somebody else told the boss but he said to stick it up your — *(He stops, stares at the tray.)* Hey! You guys licked the platter clean! How come? *(He looks at Joe.)*

JOE: Ask her. It's a long, complicated story.

SANDRA: *(absent-minded)* I was trained never to leave food on the plate.

WAITER: *(nods)* I was raised in a poor family too. *(to Joe)* The alfalfa boullion okay?

JOE: *(shakes head)* Maybe it just needs seasoning. There's no salt

THE PLIGHT OF THE LESSER SAWYER'S CRICKET

cellars on the table.

WAITER: Not allowed. But I could get it special —

SANDRA: They think salt is dangerous. Also, it's fattening. But that isn't your problem, Chauncey.

WAITER: I couldn't *eat* — everything with no salt on it. That's why I work out twice a day on the bars over at *The Body Supreme*. It just so happens I pulled a leg muscle this morning and — *(He demonstrates; Sandra politely observes.)*

SANDRA: It doesn't *look* bad —

WAITER: But when I flex it — *(He does. Joe, disinterested, pretends he sees something offstage.)*

JOE: Sandra! Look at that elderly man! He acts like he's jogging but he just stays in one place!

SANDRA: He's jogging —

WAITER: But they got to do it standing still on account of they might run into somebody. They got strict rules here —

JOE: *(an amused exchange with Sandra)* I see!

WAITER: For instance riding a bicycle in the dining room. You want to pump, you got to put it on one of those special stands like it was an Exercycle. *(nods toward deli) (pause)* See that old woman on the skateboard? She's not supposed to do that.

JOE: Then why do they let her?

WAITER: Belongs to the ruling class.

JOE: M-m-m-m?

WAITER: She's loaded. Besides. *(lowers voice and points)* You see that girl in the Bikini standing on her head? She's trying for the Guinness Book of Records. The old lady's her sponsor. *(pause)* Anyway, it's okay to walk on your hands if you don't go anywhere

SANDRA: *(politely making conversation)* She has a lovely figure.

THE PLIGHT OF THE LESSER SAWYER'S CRICKET

WAITER: Eats nothing but crushed geranium petals and apple soup! *(to Joe)* Wait'll you see her when she's right side up! Wow!

JOE: *(amused glance at Sandra)* How long do I have to wait?

WAITER: Don't know! She was doing it when I came to work.

SANDRA: She wasn't when *I* came in.

WAITER: Maybe not. But you're allowed to "take ten" to go to the John without being disqualified. *(He starts to stack dishes. He is not competent at it. Sandra helps. To Sandra:)* In my profession you can't eat all the kookie watered-down stuff — health or not. I eat only proteins. Mainly wild rabbit.

SANDRA: Wild rabbit!

JOE: Wild rabbit!

WAITER: *Jackrabbits!* Has something to do with lean, sinewy muscles. *(demonstrates)* But they're hard to get nowadays — Poison grain! The farmers've become rich, greedy plutocrats! They don't give a f — *(pause)* They don't give a darn about the ecology. That's why I got a pulled ligament.

JOE: I'm afraid I don't see the connection.

WAITER: *Quail!* I had to eat nothing but quail for a whole week!

JOE: *(savoring the idea)* Really! My God!

WAITER: Raw quail and boiled lettuce.

JOE: *(winces)* Jesus! —

SANDRA: That sounds —

WAITER: It is! But if you're trying to make the Olympic team — *(He forgets to pick up the tray and walks away with an exaggerated limp.)*

JOE: Sandra — let's settle the check and try some other place.

SANDRA: But you've an appointment!

JOE: I know. I changed my mind.

THE PLIGHT OF THE LESSER SAWYER'S CRICKET

SANDRA: What!? You were in such a hurry!

JOE: I know. All because I made another ridiculous mistake!

SANDRA: Another? *(She waits.)*

JOE: *(continued)* The appointment's for *tomorrow!*

SANDRA: It is?

JOE: Actually tomorrow afternoon.

SANDRA: But you're going to Europe tomorrow!

JOE: *(caught; pause)* Jesus! I'll have to call the airline, and —

SANDRA: But Chauncey . . . *(pause)* What a shame.

JOE: *(dismissively)* What the hell! I'm enjoying myself.

SANDRA: *(astounded)* You are! *(He nods.)* Here?

JOE: *(groping)* Well — *(pause)* Enjoying *us*, anyway.

SANDRA: That's strange. *(pause, humorously)*

JOE: *(expansive. He gets out his wallet and signals waiter.)* Sandra — Let's try Le Cafe!

SANDRA: Le Cafe! They serve milk-fed veal there.

JOE: What?

SANDRA: Veal! The Humane Society has asked the members not to patronize places that serve the milk-fed kind.

JOE: For God's sake! *We're* raised on milk — Why not calves?

SANDRA: *(embarrassed, insecure)* That's true. I — I forget just why — *(pause)* Something to do with — *(pause)* No — that's roast duck. *(pause)* There are so many important things.

JOE: We could try their Caesar salad. Anything —

SANDRA: That's not the point. If people don't boycott those places they'll go right on doing what they please! Someone's got to take a stand.

THE PLIGHT OF THE LESSER SAWYER'S CRICKET

JOE: Not me. I'm not involved — as yet.

SANDRA: Myself, then. I can't do what seems wrong — wouldn't enjoy it after I got there. *(pause) You* go!

JOE: And leave you sitting here! What kind of a guy do you think I am! *(Sandra becomes Mona Lisa again. He waits, gets an inspiration.)* Wait! Captain John's Seafood Shanty!

SANDRA: *(humbly)* Don't you understand? Fish is animal — not vegetable.

JOE: *(deflated)* Yeah. *(now guardedly)* Tokyo Gardens has millions of vegetable dishes —

SANDRA: *(lays a sympathetic hand on his)* Whales — remember?

JOE: *(reprovingly, quietly)* Sandra — Tokyo Gardens has nothing to do with Japan. It so happens the owners are third generation Americans.

SANDRA: *(shaking head)* There is a principle.

JOE: That's guilt by association! *(pause)* Look! If I refuse to drink vodka because the Russians invaded Poland —

SANDRA: Yes? *(She waits; he gives a dismissive shrug.)* It may come to that some day! *(He looks at her incredulously.)* — If millions of ordinary people suddenly took a stand! If they refuse to cooperate with wrong-doing! If all at once they wouldn't buy or use something they knew in their hearts to be harmful to any living thing — *(She stops.)* Am I grasping at straws, or aberrated? *(a silence)*

JOE: You believe in something. I envy you for that, Sandra. That doesn't mean —

SANDRA: *(moved)* Thank you. My analyst doesn't.

JOE: You wasted money on a shrink?

SANDRA: My father wasted it. Probably I didn't want to be cured.

JOE: Naturally not! This is the reason we're still sitting here. *(suddenly inspired again)* Wait! The Chinese haven't done anything

THE PLIGHT OF THE LESSER SAWYER'S CRICKET

bad! *Shanghai Gardens* —

SANDRA: *(mortified)* I can't leave here anyway!

JOE: What?

SANDRA: Malcolm. Remember? *(Joe shakes head.)* I promised we'd be here until eleven.

JOE: Then why didn't you say so? Here we're arguing about all these places —

SANDRA: I didn't have time! I got so involved —

JOE: Sandra! You let me make a fool out of myself and all the time you —

SANDRA: *(cuts in)* Out of *myself*, more likely. *(pause)* Besides, I forgot too — for a while —

JOE: *(hopefully)* You did?

SANDRA: Yes. *(brightly now)* Anyway, I thought you'd be gone before the problem came up.

JOE: *(let down again)* Problem?

SANDRA: Not male-female. He's to let me know where to meet the carpool tomorrow for the protest gathering.

JOE: Oh. *(She notes his disappointment.)* Tomorrow I was going to invite you to —

WAITER: *(arriving)* You beautiful people want something?

JOE: Changed our minds. Sorry —

WAITER: That's okay. Just holler. *(Exits, forgetting to limp.)*

SANDRA: You were asking about tomorrow? But you have that business appointment.

JOE: No, no. I'm talking about tomorrow *night*.

SANDRA: Oh! I could get back in time if nobody gets arrested.

JOE: Hey! It so happens a friend gave me two twenty dollar seats

61

THE PLIGHT OF THE LESSER SAWYER'S CRICKET

	for the National Rodeo!
SANDRA:	*(agonized)* Oh, no! That's where we're going tomorrow!
JOE:	What?
SANDRA:	We're going to throw a picket line across the entrance. Cruel, illegal treatment of animals!
JOE:	In a rodeo for God's sake! What in hell can be wrong with a clean, wholesome Western tradition?
SANDRA:	*(quietly)* Everything.
JOE:	*What!* Because some fool cowboy is willing to get himself busted up to make a few bucks? That's *his* business!
SANDRA:	That's part of it. But people shouldn't pay to watch it! They shouldn't be *allowed* to watch!
JOE:	Sandra! Where have you been! What about auto racing! Boxing! Football! Even mountain climbing! It's part of human nature to take risks!
SANDRA:	I'm not stopping them! I'm just saying that nobody should watch — any more than watching an execution! *(pause)* The issue is the animals — *they* didn't volunteer! They're only trying to protect themselves.
JOE:	Baloney! Ever watch a bullfight?
SANDRA:	Of course not! The bulls are prodded, goaded, tortured first. Naturally they attack!
JOE:	Ever seen a rider kicked by a horse? It hurts! Or stomped by one of your peace-loving cows?
SANDRA:	It's the same thing! The animals are all psyched up by barbs — electric prodders — sharp burrs under the saddle!
JOE:	Who says?
SANDRA:	The humane investigators. The reports are shocking. *(She reaches for another pamphlet.)*
JOE:	*(shakes head)* Never mind. I'll take your word for it.

THE PLIGHT OF THE LESSER SAWYER'S CRICKET

(A long silence. Joe looks around the room. We hear sounds — dishes, utensils, voices. He is restless, but there is nothing to say. He gets out his cigarettes, lays them on the table.)

          Illegal, of course?

SANDRA: *(nods)* But somebody is smoking pot. I smell it.

JOE: How about coffee? That illegal too?

SANDRA: *(nods)* Herb tea of course. Twenty-three varieties.

JOE: That's an idea! *Jasmine.*

SANDRA: That's a no-no. Any tea made from tea leaves has contingencies.

JOE: Sandra — how long do we have to wait for your friend?

SANDRA: He's unusually late.

JOE: It's ten forty-five now. Can't you call him and say —

SANDRA: *(gesture of helplessness)* He's been *disconnected. (Joe looks blank.)* For refusing to pay the telephone tax.

JOE: M-m-m-m-m? *What?*

SANDRA: *War* tax. A part of your bill goes for national defense. Malcolm has been deducting that part and they caught up with him.

JOE: *(defeated; now soberly)* What happens Thursday, Sandra?

SANDRA: Thursday? Don't you have to be in Europe?

JOE: No. *(flustered)* Changed my mind.

SANDRA: Oh! *(sadly)* Unfortunately —

JOE: *(fatalistically)* I know. You've got to save the rattlesnakes.

SANDRA: It's almost that bad. There's a tiny minnow that lives in waterholes in the desert. It's called — Do you really want to hear about it?

JOE: The pupfish!

THE PLIGHT OF THE LESSER SAWYER'S CRICKET

SANDRA: *(astonished, delighted)* Right! Somebody's actually heard of it!

JOE: Saw it on television. *(She is more than astonished.)* The Pirate's game was cancelled. Before I could change channels —

SANDRA: So now you know what happens Thursday!

JOE: I do?

SANDRA: Endangered species, right? *(pause)* Why did you change your plans about Thursday?

JOE: *(groping)* Because I — *(pause)* The whole thing was a mistake in judgement.

SANDRA: Judgement?

JOE: *(awkwardly)* The person I made the appointment with — I changed my mind.

SANDRA: So you're not going to Europe because you don't want to see them?

JOE: Yes! I mean, no! I mean — *(pause)* I'll tell you later. Meanwhile, which endangered species were you talking about?

SANDRA: The pupfish! They've lived in brackish water where nothing else can exist since prehistoric times. Now, farmers are lowering the water lev — *(stops)* But you saw the program! Have you forgotten?

JOE: I didn't have time! There was a basketball game on Channel Twelve. *(pause)* — So I'm a bastard.

SANDRA: Just plead Nolo Contendre again. Anyway, a group of us are going to stage a sit-in.

JOE: Wait! That's way out on the California desert!

SANDRA: No. Department of the Interior downtown. One pond is already dried up. By actual count only twenty-seven are living in water capable of sustaining life.

(Unconsciously, she takes a long drink from her glass. Joe soberly does same. She frowns, examines glass again.)

Chlorinated.

JOE: You already mentioned that. *(smiles)* — But capable of sustaining life.

SANDRA: I'm not so sure about that.

JOE: *Sandra* —

SANDRA: Who knows? Sooner or later some brilliant scientist will find that it does more harm than good! *(pause)* For all I know, chlorination may cause *cancer*.

JOE: Oh, no!

SANDRA: Practically everything does nowadays. *(pauses, waits)*

JOE: Go on —

SANDRA: Never mind — just one of my subjective declamations.

JOE: But I *want* to hear! I want to know everything! Good, bad, or preposterous!

SANDRA: Why?

JOE: Don't you know why?

SANDRA: *(demurely)* I think I'd be wiser to retain part of me for myself.

JOE: Why?

SANDRA: Instinct. When something is dear or precious you don't want to risk destroying it.

JOE: You've risked a helluva lot so far and survived —

SANDRA: *(wise smile)* So have you! More than you'll ever realize.

JOE: I get it. — I think. *(pause)* Anyway, both of us are survivalists so far — despite a hostile environment —

SANDRA: *(soberly)* Yes.

VOICE: *(a man; calling from the deli section)* Hey, Dwayne! Dwayne Warren!

(Joe reacts, stiffens, looks toward deli. Sandra has paid no attention, but

THE PLIGHT OF THE LESSER SAWYER'S CRICKET

discovers that the caller is addressing Joe.)

SANDRA: That man seems to be calling you, Chauncey.

JOE: *(grimly)* Yeah. *(calls)* Hi, Tom —

VOICE: What's up! Trying to regain your lost health?

JOE: *(inhibited)* Something like that.

VOICE: I don't blame you! Well, I see you're busy! Give my regards to the pheasants!

(Joe waves cheerily. Sandra avoids looking at him, but she is smiling.)

JOE: Um — that was Tom.

SANDRA: *(enjoying)* I know. But who are you?

JOE: *(pulls self together to face it all; humble)* Sandra — I lied to you about everything except for one thing. And I haven't brought that up yet —

SANDRA: Yes. Maybe it won't be necessary, Dwayne.

JOE: *(searching, but she reveals nothing)* M-m-m-m-m?

SANDRA: What did your friend mean about the pheasants?

JOE: *(soberly)* The hunting season opens next week.

SANDRA: I know all about that.

JOE: Did you know I'm not going to go? I gave it up.

SANDRA: *(pleased)* How nice! When did you decide that?

JOE: *(sheepish)* About eight minutes ago.

SANDRA: Then I won't see you there — I was supposed to go with a group that plans to scare the birds away from the hunters.

JOE: You said "was" —

SANDRA: I know. Second thoughts — It doesn't seem quite right to — *(stops)* — and yet, if someone doesn't make a start — *(pause)* I'm always embarrassed about embarrassing people in a personal way. *(pause)* Do you know what I mean? I don't! But

THE PLIGHT OF THE LESSER SAWYER'S CRICKET

some confrontations may do more harm than good —

JOE: Knowing hunters as I do, you might accidentally get shot on purpose, too.

SANDRA: That is of no concern, naturally.

JOE: Naturally. *(He plants an unlighted cigarette in his mouth and talks through it.)* Sandra — now that you've found out everything about me —

SANDRA: Everything? I only know you tell more lies than I but aren't as good at it! *(pause)* And that you're not an FBI man or a private detective.

JOE: Suppose I was? Would it make any difference?

SANDRA: Not the least bit. I've nothing to hide — from anyone.

JOE: All right. What about the part of yourself you decided to hold back?

SANDRA: You mean very personal things —

JOE: *(nods)* You see, I've a theory about boy-meets-girl relationships. *Find out the worst first!* Then, if there's anything left —

SANDRA: Which one of us shall cast the first stone?

JOE: M-m-m-m-m?

SANDRA: *Bible. (She waits; Joe doesn't get it.)* Shall I start first with the worst? *(Joe nods.)* To begin with, I don't believe in medicine, doctors, germs, analysts — *(She waits; Joe pretends to be unimpressed.)* Don't just sit there, Dwayne! Say something!

JOE: Okay. *Jesus Christ!*

SANDRA: Correct. Jesus didn't believe in those things either.

JOE: What happens if you get sick?

SANDRA: I don't know. I try to make it a point not to.

JOE: Yeah. I had a Christian Scientist aunt.

67

THE PLIGHT OF THE LESSER SAWYER'S CRICKET

SANDRA: Well?

JOE: She died.

SANDRA: I've heard somewhere that doctors also die. Of course, there's no way to prove it.

JOE: Okay, okay. But why do you go to places like this?

SANDRA: Not for health —

JOE: But you nibble away on all those weird things normal people wouldn't touch.

SANDRA: What makes you think so? For millions of years people ate anything and everything they could find. In fact, humans started out as vegetarians before — *(Joe pretends to hide a yawn.)* Before they discovered veal scallopini. *(pause)* Enough?

JOE: But you seem to have an inordinate amount of faith in alfalfa sprouts, like everybody else nowadays.

SANDRA: And a little mustard seed.

JOE: What?

SANDRA: *Bible,* again.

JOE: I haven't seen the Good Book since Sunday School. What about —

SANDRA: Mustard seed? It's a parable regarding faith. To me, everything is faith healing — Doctors, voodoo, pills, rabbit's feet, God, vitamins — or just some personal belief — *(Looks at him, waiting.)* Well — ?

JOE: You make me feel lonely. Go on, please.

SANDRA: My African friend Rollo — *(pause)* Romboto —? *(pause)* Anyway, he thinks Americans are masochists. If something tastes terrible or hurts we think it's good for us.

JOE: I feel that way about this stuff. If you're sick enough to eat it you must be half dead anyway.

THE PLIGHT OF THE LESSER SAWYER'S CRICKET

VOICE: *(calling)* Sandy! *(Sandra waves.)* We can't go tomorrow night. Ed cracked up his VW again. *(Sandra acknowledges.)*

JOE: As you were saying —

SANDRA: *(suddenly staring at the potted plant next to Joe)* Wait! There's a spider headed for your coat!

(Joe reacts, dodging away. She quickly goes over to the plant. Joe arms himself with one of the pamphlets.)

JOE: Where?

SANDRA: Right here! *(He puts on his glasses and tries to see it.)* Wait! Don't hurt it!

JOE: What?

SANDRA: I'll just do this — *(She takes her finger across the strand of web and skillfully transfers it to the other side of plant.)*

JOE: *(humorously, but ashamed of his reaction)* You saved my life!

SANDRA: Two lives. It's against the rules to kill something unless you're going to eat it, you know — *(pause)* I should have taken it outside where it belongs.

JOE: *(glancing doubtfully at plant)* As far as I'm concerned, it would be a lot healthier out there.

SANDRA: But doesn't know it, of course. *(She starts to sit, then picks a leaf off the plant and nibbles on it experimentally.)*

JOE: Why're you doing that?

SANDRA: Because I've never tried Spittusporium. *(Frowns, daintily removes leaf with Kleenex.)* — Not good, not bad. Better than the hors d'oeuvres, though.

WAITER: *(comes up)* Everything okay now? I told Marge about those bugs. She says they can't spray until after everybody leaves. Some folks might object —

JOE: To killing them or polluting the air?

WAITER: Both. You got potted plants, you got pests? Right?

THE PLIGHT OF THE LESSER SAWYER'S CRICKET

SANDRA: Then they shouldn't have plants indoors. The insects think it's their natural home — They have just as much right to be here as we do —

WAITER: *(noncommital)* Well — *(He leaves, flexing en route.)*

SANDRA: That's another thing I don't believe in. Body building. Workouts, Keeping fit. To me it's narcissism.

JOE: But it looks good. To some people —

SANDRA: I think if you're undersexed a beautiful body could be quite important.

JOE: Oh? To me, yours is beautiful but that doesn't mean I'm undersexed. *(pause)* Or oversexed.

SANDRA: Thank you. But I don't swing the Indian clubs in a gym. I wouldn't waste my time that way.

JOE: How, then?

SANDRA: Doesn't Kharma determine your genes? Anyway, normal daily life is my fitness program — washing windows, waxing the floor, shaking out rugs and climbing fences to get arrested — *(pause)* And partly from avoiding being over thirty.

JOE: Yeah. That helps, doesn't it?

SANDRA: Always. But it shouldn't, of course.

JOE: No! I've a theory I made up all by myself. For millions of years most women died of old age in their twenties. It's natural for men to mate with young girls in order to carry on the race.

SANDRA: Are you sure you invented that? I seem to have read it in whatsisname's sociology text. Which has since been refuted —

JOE: Of course I made it up! You know I never read anything. *(He turns to look for spider.)* How's our little friend doing?

SANDRA: He's still there — smiling appreciatively.

JOE: Sandra, we never got to finish about killing pests. What do you do about flies, ants, moths?

THE PLIGHT OF THE LESSER SAWYER'S CRICKET

SANDRA: If I can't shoo them away I get tickled.

JOE: What about the ones that bite or sting?

SANDRA: Well — sometimes it's an eye for an eye. But I try to avoid circumstances where it might occur. Next question?

JOE: The prosecution rests.

SANDRA: Good. I feel as though I'm getting to know everything about you. You don't read, but you're capable of thinking whenever it's absolutely necessary.

JOE: Much obliged. But I try not to let it get in the way when something important happens.

SANDRA: I see.

JOE: For example, I agree wth you about people who can't lift a finger around the house — can't bend down to put a dish on the lowest shelf, or reach up and whisk off a cobweb. But if they have to drive across town and pay money to work themselves into a frazzle in a gym —!

SANDRA: Did I say that? What I meant is the waste of time and energy that's needed for so many urgent, worthwhile things.

JOE: Right. The only reason I attend workout classes is because I don't have time for recreation.

SANDRA: Oh.

JOE: That's why I had to sell the boat.

SANDRA: Oh.

JOE: Speaking of boat, Sandra! It just occured to me that I have some surplus cash on hand. *(pause, guardedly)* I was thinking about your problem — bail money.

SANDRA: Oh? What brought that up?

JOE: You. But there it is — the cash.

SANDRA: I see. *(pause)* It was there a half hour ago too.

JOE: Yeah. But *we* weren't.

THE PLIGHT OF THE LESSER SAWYER'S CRICKET

SANDRA: That's very brave. And kind. But I never accept money from friends or enemies. Much less, people who think they're involved — Or if *I* might be involved.

JOE: *(eagerly)* Well — are you —

VOICE: *(a woman; interrupting)* Hey, Sandy! I thought you didn't have time for hanky-pank!

SANDRA: *(calling)* I don't. *(indicating Joe)* — Ask him!

JOE: *(calling)* Never a spare moment!

VOICE: See you at the vigil —

SANDRA: *(to Joe)* Her husband just left her.

JOE: *(dryly)* Too many pupfish —?

SANDRA: No. He followed his guru to India.

JOE: You seem to have a lot of unusual friends.

SANDRA: Acquaintances.

JOE: And they don't seem too upset despite their problems.

SANDRA: Whatsername isn't, even though she has a lawsuit over her car accident, and foreclosure on the house and three mixed-up children. On the other hand, my father spends his time traveling all over the world, owns two townhouses and three mountain or lake homes and feels depressed because his Mercedes-Benz agencies are only bringing in seven hundred thousand a year . . .

JOE: So you're another of these poor little rich girls. I kind of suspected it.

SANDRA: Oh. *(pause)* Anyway, my point is that animals are merely trying to survive whereas people are exterminating or trampling them because they're in our way —

JOE: *(absently)* Yeah, I agree. *(now interestedly)* Where is your father's agency?

SANDRA: One's in Greenwich, Connecticut. The other is —

THE PLIGHT OF THE LESSER SAWYER'S CRICKET

JOE: Hey! That's where I got *my* car!

SANDRA: Really? So you're another poor little rich boy. A Mercedes —?

JOE: No. Cadillac off his used car lot.

VOICE: *(a man; calling)* Hey! Saint Joan!

JOE: Oh, no. Not another one!

SANDRA: *(dutifuly calls and waves)* Hi! I thought you were supposed to be at the swim-in!

VOICE: I *was*. But the Doc said I got to take my allergy shots.

SANDRA: *(to Joe)* That's whatsisname — *(pause)* I'm terrible about names —

JOE: *(dryly)* Not Malcolm whatsisname —

SANDRA: Oh no! *(indicating caller)* He's the one who was picked up with the Berrigan brothers. *(pause)* When they — when they — *(pause)* I forgot what it was they did —

JOE: Anyway, what's a swim-in?

SANDRA: *(resignedly)* Polaris *submarines!*

JOE: Okay. Polaris submarines —

SANDRA: Every time they launch a new one we stage a swim-in. *Protest* —

JOE: *(confused)* They swim along beside it? The sub? Why?

SANDRA: In front! They swim in front to obstruct its passage. War-protest. *(Joe whistles.)* But instead of marching they swim.

JOE: *(cheerily)* And of course the captain surrenders — *(more seriously)* But it *is* dangerous —

SANDRA: No. The harbor police or coast guard snatch everybody out of the water.

JOE: So — nothing gained, nothing lost.

SANDRA: It brings it to the attention of the public. *(pause, smiles*

73

THE PLIGHT OF THE LESSER SAWYER'S CRICKET

mischievously at him) Some of the public.

JOE: The ones who don't watch the ball game. *(pause)* Sandra — why did that guy call you Saint Joan?

SANDRA: It's a perverse joke. He knows I detest Joan of Arc.

JOE: What?

SANDRA: To me she represents a spoiled, ego-oriented little groupie.

JOE: You mean underage Women's Lib. I get it.

SANDRA: Worse. A pubescent cheerleader goading men to go out and kill each other. I hate it.

JOE: At least she was willing to die for a cause. *(pause)* I'm not.

SANDRA: Nor I. But why shouldn't she be willing? After telling everybody else to go out and get killed for some stupid patriotic honor? *(pause)* I'm not vain enough to think I'm more important as a dead martyr than a live protester.

JOE: I like that. Of course you do have a special way of looking at everything — I never know what you're going to say next.

SANDRA: One of my friends says I'm predictably unpredictable.

JOE: Tell him I think that's a good prediction.

SANDRA: *She.* She's the one Henry's involved with just now, although he insists he's gay.

JOE: Oh, sure! When a girl dates a cute young guy — or not so cute — she always has to say "He's wonderful! Really a charming, worthwhile guy. But gay of course —"

SANDRA: Well — maybe he is!

JOE: And maybe he'll switch, just to prove something to himself. *(She attentively waits.)* — Don Juan! The priest who wants to entice some girl into raping him.

SANDRA: The feminine mystique! Curiosity —

JOE: I know. And it scares me.

THE PLIGHT OF THE LESSER SAWYER'S CRICKET

SANDRA: And men scare women who hope for too much. *(pause)* I think you're too charismatic to be so skeptical —

JOE: And you're too damn attractive to go around saving sea lions and horses. Even with the no-nonsense look.

SANDRA: You mean cosmetics. But I do believe in using make-up! *(She pats one of the shopping bags.)* Even though it's terribly expensive — the kind I have to use.

JOE: Yeah. A wise woman's most important investment.

SANDRA: Agreed! But the kinds I use cost double because they are approved —

JOE: M-m-m-m-m?

SANDRA: By the Animal Protective League! *(She starts to rummage through pamphlets.)* The major cosmetics manufacturers have been using rabbits and other animals for testing! *(She falls silent to concentrate on search for proper brochure.)*

JOE: Never mind, for God's sake.

SANDRA: I *do* mind! If the eye makeup or rouge blinds the animal or burns it, they can't pass the human health standards.

JOE: *(impatient again)* Okay, okay!

SANDRA: So I have to use a special kind that's not tested on animals.

JOE: So *you* are the guinea pig.

SANDRA: No — it's tested on other humans first. That's why it costs so much.

(A silence. The dining room background noise then becomes louder, with someone trying to play "Greensleeves" on the recorder.)

JOE: As they say, everybody's allowed to do his own thing nowadays. I should have brought my violin along.

SANDRA: I almost believe you're half serious.

JOE: My wife doesn't think so. *(He watches out of the corner of his eye for Sandra's reaction to this. There is none. He is part-*

ly relieved, partly disappointed.) She's into classical music. In a vicarious way — committees — fund-raising —

SANDRA: My mother did that — especially the latter, which is more important. Of course most of the money was my father's and now he thinks *he* needs funds.

JOE: And the poor little rich girl solves her problems with buses and carpools.

SANDRA: And her Datsun sportscar sits in her garage because of a species of whale — *(He waits, confused.)* The Japanese treaty, remember?

JOE: Yeah, Anyway, it must make your father happy.

SANDRA: What do you mean?

JOE: Your one-man stand against foreign competition. Tokyo Joe.

SANDRA: He doesn't know. It would hurt him. Birthday present —

JOE: A Japanese car? Why not a Mercedes?

SANDRA: I refused. Subjective — To me they're nothing but a status symbol — noisy — boxy — and always in the repair shop —

JOE: Jesus! Now I've heard everything. But at least they're not murdering sharks or poisoning the rattlesnakes.

SANDRA: Poisoning the air, though, with their diesel —

JOE: Sandra — according to you, everything's *(pause)* unhealthy — controversial — bad — inhumane —

SANDRA: I don't want to sound that way. It makes it difficult to have a rapport. Sometimes I feel alienated — no close friends —

VOICE: Hey, Sandy! Right on! *(She offers a wan acknowledgement.)*

JOE: You seem to be doing all right! *(pause)* — I have complicated problems too, Sandra —

SANDRA: But mine are of my own doing. Up until I left Vassar there were a mother and a father. Why would I give up a career job because of a cricket! Or crusade for a marine monster

THE PLIGHT OF THE LESSER SAWYER'S CRICKET

I've never even seen?

JOE: *(gallantly)* Because you had to!

SANDRA: But you didn't.

JOE: *(soberly, significantly)* Maybe I will have to, Sandra —

SANDRA: *(pleased but unconvinced)* No. Maybe temporarily — a romantic fling with an ideal — and then back to normalcy.

JOE: *(hurting)* You're sure about that?

(Sandra affixes him with her noncommital smile again.)

Half the time when I ask you a question I feel as though Mona Lisa's sitting on the judge's bench.

SANDRA: *(amused)* All right. *Not* sure.

JOE: *(encouraged; exploratively now)* It would be funny if we fell in — *(pause)* if we became involved — and switched roles! I went crusading for the hummingbirds and you stayed home and ironed shirts —

(Sandra waits with her quixotic smile.)

Does that mean "yes" or "no"?

(They are interrupted by a sudden silence followed by excited voices. The police have entered the delicatessen section.)

VOICE: *(a police officer's)* Freeze! Stay where you are! *(A scream and shouts. Sandra and Joe tense and stare toward the commotion.)*

VOICE: Are you Andrew Langley Romans? Show me your ID.

VOICE: I am. But I don't carry a wallet.

SANDRA: It's Andy whatsisname! He refused to register!

JOE: What?

SANDRA: *(stands up but doesn't move from table)* The draft.

VOICE: We have orders to take you in, sir.

(Sound of a body falling. A chair is knocked over and dishes rattle.)

77

THE PLIGHT OF THE LESSER SAWYER'S CRICKET

SANDRA: *(almost pleased)* He's going limp!

JOE: Going *where?*

SANDRA: Limp. Refusing to cooperate.

VOICE: You're not going to pull that stuff again!?

JOE: He's lying flat on the floor!

SANDRA: *(amused)* He's too fat to carry! They'll have to drag him by the feet.

VOICES: *(cheering)* Right on, Andy... Make 'em work for it!... Wow!... That's throwing your weight around ... *(laughter)*

JOE: All in all, the cops're being pretty nice about it. *(pause)* Resisting arrest —

SANDRA: No. There's a legal difference between resisting arrest and non-cooperation. He knows the difference and so do they. And there are plenty of eager witnesses.

VOICES: *(cheers, boos)*

JOE: They're trying to drag him! Good way to clean the floor *(pause)* — How come Saint Joan doesn't go over to lead the cheering section?

SANDRA: There are plenty of enthusiastic witnesses. I *would* tell them I'm a witness if they used excessive force. *(pause)* Otherwise, why harass police officers? They've enough troubles.

JOE: The mob's following him out the door. Why?

SANDRA: *(almost bitterly)* Because they have nothing better to do.

VOICES: *(more cheering, farther away)* See you in the lockup, Andy... Try not to be late for the Pentagon mobilization... Hey! Don't go on a hunger strike!... your jacket needs brushing off... be sure to write...

JOE: *(marvelling)* I never realized cops and robbers games could be so much fun!

THE PLIGHT OF THE LESSER SAWYER'S CRICKET

SANDRA: Sometimes I suspect the police enjoy it more than anybody. After all, it's a safe, pleasant way to earn your salary. *(She notices that Joe has glanced at his watch again.)* What time is it, Dwayne?

JOE: Almost eleven.

SANDRA: I have to leave soon.

JOE: *(stunned)* What?!

SANDRA: Our engagement was only for dinner — remember?

JOE: But we haven't *had* dinner!

SANDRA: I'm sorry. Had I known — naturally —

JOE: Goddamit! You're being perverse! Everything's different now!

SANDRA: *(quietly hushed)* Yes. I know —

JOE: Well?

SANDRA: I still have to be at City Hall by midnight — there's a special meeting. The People's Park committee.

JOE: Fuck the park! Which is more important — us or them?

SANDRA: I agree it doesn't seem important just now. *(She starts to get up.)*

JOE: Then sit!

SANDRA: *(shakes head)* I always keep promises. I can't help it. *(waits)* — It's not like I was going off to the wars — or Europe — If anything is there — won't it keep?

JOE: Sandra! If you walk out of this room without —

SANDRA: Only to the restroom to freshen up a bit. All right?

JOE: *(slightly relieved)* Okay. What about your friends?

SANDRA: I only promised to wait until ten. *(She exits left stage taking shopping bag.)*

(Joe fidgets restlessly. Swelling sounds of crowd returning inside. They sing

THE PLIGHT OF THE LESSER SAWYER'S CRICKET

"We Shall Overcome" again. The voices are angry, excited, but not sorrowful—almost jubilant.)

VOICES: ... He *was* bleeding ... That was already there ... chili sauce! ... When they grabbed his ankles I saw him wince ... Sure! He's an actor isn't he? ... No, I think it was real! ... It'll even be realer on the way to the jail ... That's why I wanted them to take *me* in too—*witnesses* ... The police aren't so dumb as they act sometimes ... etc.

(Joe listens intently. He notices that their attention is focused on one of the speakers. He quickly gets out his cigarettes and bends down in back of the table. He takes several frantic drags, watches the deli and takes a few more, keeping his cigarette close to the floor. The waiter arrives, gliding up on silent roller skates.)

WAITER: Hi!

(Joe, having neither seen nor heard the waiter until now, instinctively ducks back as the apparition seems about to run him down.)

Remember I had a pulled leg muscle? *(Joe nods, grinding out cigarette and sitting back.)* I tole Marge and she said why don't you put on roller skates and get around faster! She said it! You guys care for dessert or did she cut out? *(pause)* There's a cactus souffle made with cabbage sugar and crushed olive pits —

JOE: Just the check I guess. We're running late.

WAITER: I didn't mean to ignore you so long. *(He glides to and fro.)* There was this raid — *(indicates deli)*

JOE: I know.

WAITER: Like, I tole the manager the or-doovers stunk.

JOE: *(preoccupied)* What did he say?

WAITER: *You're fired.*

JOE: M-m-m-m-m?

WAITER: You're fired. He tole me to go to the cashier and draw out

THE PLIGHT OF THE LESSER SAWYER'S CRICKET

                my chickenshit twenty-three dollars and fifty cents after closing.

JOE: I'm sorry. I hope it had nothing to do with our — nothing to do with you —

WAITER: No way! Ruling class versus the worker! Some stool pigeon tole him I'm a Marxist and he got a tight asshole. Actually I'm a revisionist Trotskyite except I don't go for what they did in Poland although I was actually born in Czechoslovakia —

JOE: *(getting up)* Will you excuse me while I make a call?

WAITER: Sure, comrade, and I'll get the bill.

(Joe dials on phone. Waiter pirouettes a few circles and we hear complaints and cheers from offstage.)

VOICES: Wow . . . Watch it . . . Don't let Helen see that . . .

JOE: *(on phone)* Harold? Stevie. *(pause)* I don't have time to talk about it now. *(pause)* Listen — is anybody sleeping aboard your boat tonight? *(pause)* You never *know*? *(pause)* Orgies! I never *did* really go for orgies. *(pause)* That doesn't mean I *enjoyed* it! *(pause)* Look — can you call the MacIntoshes and tell them you already promised the boat? *(pause)* You don't *have* to tell them who it's for! *(pause)* All right — make up a name! *(pause)*

(The waiter skates up, waits.)

                Just say a friend dropped in from Europe. Why do they have to be so goddammed inquisitive —? *(pause)* They do? Since when? *(pause)* I see. *(pause)* Just because they're paying the slip rent doesn't mean — *(pause)* Look! Your friend Chauncey just came in from the hot desert and wants to cool off! *Chauncey* — Chauncey Baxter. Okay? *(pause)* You promise? *(pause)* Thanks, Harold — I knew I could count on you — bye. *(Joe heads for table.)*

WAITER: Hey! You're in luck! The boss isn't going to permit you to pay the bill!

THE PLIGHT OF THE LESSER SAWYER'S CRICKET

JOE: Oh?

WAITER: On account of you guys insulted the food! But you got to promise never to come back.

JOE: Okay. I'm leaving town anyway.

WAITER: *(lowering voice)* One thing's kookie, though — He asked how come you guys licked up every scrap if it's so lousy. *(Joe waits.)* I tole him like, I throwed it in the garbage. I was already fired any —

(The waiter stops. His attention is caught by an action offstage in the deli.)

What's everybody staring at?

(Joe stands to get a better look. Their heads follow the progress of Sandra across the area. Joe tenses.)

Wow! *(whistles)* Who's that! Hey! She's coming here! — That isn't the same lady you was with who went to the can?

JOE: *(miffed)* Of course!

WAITER: Wow! It's amazing what a little gussying-up will do for a plain little chick! *(whistles again)* Wow!

JOE: *(brooding over the remark)* Yeah. Mind picking up the dirty dishes?

WAITER: Right on! *(He glides up and starts stacking but is deliberately methodical, malingering.)*

(Sandra comes on stage. Whatever she is wearing, she looks "patrician," whether or not it is from a thrift shop. She stops a few feet from Joe. His expression is one of reverence, anguish, desire, pride, insecurity. Sandra appears completely unselfconscious of her appearance, but curious that it has such an effect on Joe. Joe seats her and sits. A long pause. The waiter wonders why they haven't touched or embraced or spoken.)

Hi! How do you like my roller skates?

SANDRA: *(long pause)* M-m-m-m-m? *(pause)* Oh, fine.

JOE: *(hoarsely)* Sandra — *(He stops, clears throat.)*

THE PLIGHT OF THE LESSER SAWYER'S CRICKET

SANDRA: Yes, Dwayne?

(He reacts to the name and upsets glass and dishes. Waiter glides quickly over and straightens things.)

JOE: Look, Sandra, I don't know what to say —

SANDRA: *(smiles)* Then don't.

JOE: You can't run off and leave me here now.

SANDRA: Now? Because I look like the girl at the Albergs'?

JOE: That makes no difference.

SANDRA: *(compassionately)* Of course it does! It made a difference earlier tonight. It'll always make a difference.

(The waiter weaves in and out gathering dishes.)

JOE: *(irritated)* Never mind. We have to leave.

SANDRA: *(shakes head)* No! I just found my ride won't be ready for several minutes.

JOE: I got a better idea — I'll drive you down to the City Hall.

SANDRA: I already made arrangements with Henry.

JOE: *(angrily)* Just now?

SANDRA: Last week. We have to plan strategy for the committee before we get there.

(The waiter glides confidently but precariously away with the stacked tray.)

JOE: Afterwards. I could pick you up —

SANDRA: Afterwards — *(pause)* Oh, Dwayne — The Sierra Club has a walk-in at Echo Lake. We'll drive all night and get there in time to —

JOE: Never mind.

SANDRA: *(sincerely)* I'd ask you to come along but we already have eleven people for whatsisname's van —

THE PLIGHT OF THE LESSER SAWYER'S CRICKET

JOE: We could split it up! Two cars —

SANDRA: I thought of that but Kenny wouldn't like it.

JOE: Kenny? It's *not* male-female business!

SANDRA: Was. But he doesn't know it yet

JOE: Jesus.

SANDRA: I feel the same way. None of these things seem very important right now.

JOE: *(somewhat mollified)* What about Wednesday?

SANDRA: *(slowly shakes head)* Dog Pound. The animal shelters are selling —

JOE: Sandra, you just said these things don't seem so important —

SANDRA: They might if you're a dog or a cat!

JOE: I have *two* dogs. I don't let them run around loose, though.

SANDRA: *(wistfully)* I've no pets — not even a goldfish.

JOE: Oh? And you an animal lover? Why?

SANDRA: It's not fair — keeping them locked up. Or leaving them alone all the time.

JOE: *(rebuffed)* Thanks a lot. *(pause; now demandingly)* Okay! Friday then. God damn it!

SANDRA: My day in court. I can't get out of that.

JOE: I'll get my lawyer to attend to it — the bail too.

SANDRA: *(shakes head forlornly)* Principle of the thing. But thanks.

JOE: *(anguished, pleadingly)* Sandra, you don't seem to understand about love. With me it's all or nothing! I want to be with you every minute! I want to *own* you, damn it! I'm getting a divorce, and —

SANDRA: *(astonished)* Why would you do a thing like that!

(There is a piercing scream, shouting, oaths. The waiter has collided with

THE PLIGHT OF THE LESSER SAWYER'S CRICKET

someone and the tray of dishes crashes.)

VOICES: . . . those fucking roller skates out of here! . . . She's okay . . . Idiotic asshole! . . . sure, and I'll say it again . . . etc.

SANDRA: *(long, silent pause. The mood has been destroyed. She gathers her shopping bags and stands.)* Well —

JOE: *(outraged)* You're not going to just walk out saying "well!"

SANDRA: What more is there to say? We know how we feel —

JOE: But I can't call you — you — you're disconnected.

SANDRA: I'll call *you. (She starts to go.)*

JOE: *(pleased but doubting)* How do I know you will?

SANDRA: Because I keep promises. Because I want to.

JOE: *(thrilled but concerned)* Really? *(pause)* — But not at the office. Our secretary's the nosey type.

SANDRA: I see. What about your house?

JOE: I'm hardly ever there. But if the wife or kids answer you could tell them you're from the insurance company and —

SANDRA: I won't lie. You know that.

JOE: Jesus!

SANDRA: *(humorously)* I'll just tell them that Chauncey and Joe are getting a divorce.

JOE: *(bitterly)* Ha, ha.

SANDRA: No. I'd introduce myself and ask when or where I can reach you.

VOICE: *(calling, demanding)* Sandra! Get your ass out here!

SANDRA: *(waves, nods)* Coming! *(to Joe)* —I'm not certain many people *deserve* my morality.

JOE: Now you're really getting wierd!

SANDRA: As I said, you know very little about me.

THE PLIGHT OF THE LESSER SAWYER'S CRICKET

JOE: So what! I know how I feel! Call it chemistry or Kharma, like you say, but I know one thing — if a beautiful nude girl hopped into my bed I'd push her out! *(Sandra is Mona Lisa again.)* — Why? Because there's only one person on earth! I'm immune! Neuter gender. And you're —

SANDRA: *(cuts in)* There's a cure for that! *Time!*

JOE: You don't even know what I'm talking about! I've never felt like this in my life before! — Have you?

SANDRA: Four times.

JOE: I'm not talking about sex.

SANDRA: Nor am I. Sex I've had dozens of times.

JOE: Jesus Christ!

VOICE: *(calling)* Henry says to meet him out in the truck. Okay?

SANDRA: *(nods, starts walking)* Well — goodbye — Dwayne —

JOE: Wait! Goddammit! *(She continues walking.)* Sandra! Look! *(She turns, waits.)* Look — don't bother to call the house.

SANDRA: I didn't intend to.

JOE: But you promised!

SANDRA: I lied. *(She turns and starts walking.)*

JOE: *(furiously, but as though to himself, loud enough for her to hear)* Okay. Go fuck yourself. *(He turns and slumps into chair with his back to her. She stops, her back to him.)*

SANDRA: By the way — I'm looking for a ride to Green Valley tomorrow night. *(Joe sits erect, surprised she's still there.)* — My friend's car got wrecked.

(They remain back to back for the remainder of the scene. Joe listens.)

I wonder if you happened to know of anybody who's going that way. It's very important to me —

JOE: *(knocks some of the tableware to the floor. He pauses, looks*

THE PLIGHT OF THE LESSER SAWYER'S CRICKET

up at ceiling.) It just so happens I may . . .

SANDRA: It'll be a rough trip if they're not used to hiking-in and sleeping under the stars — if the acid rain doesn't blot them out.

JOE: *(to the fourth wall)* The person I have in mind would put up with a lot if it's a worthwhile cause.

SANDRA: That depends. The "cause" is an insignificant little insect that chirps in the night. An unusual group of humans hope to save him from being drowned by the Hooton Dam . . .

JOE: I see. *(clearing his throat)* — It so happens this person is already obligated to take his children on a nature walk Tuesday and Wednesday. Might he be allowed to bring them along?

SANDRA: The more warm bodies, the better for the TV reporters — *(A silence. We see Joe wince.) (pause)* — That is, we *hope* the media will cover it.

JOE: *(winces again)* My friend's wife doesn't go for all these demonstrations and publicity stunts. If she happens to see it on the screen —

SANDRA: I hope you're wrong! She should be glad her kids — the new generation — are doing something about the environment! *(pause)* As a matter of fact, several other children want to come if your friend's car is big enough.

(They remain stationary, Joe facing the left wall, Sandra facing the right wall.)

SANDRA: Anyway, if he decides to go, we'll be here at eight-thirty tomorrow night —

(Sandra walks offstage. Music: garbled voices rendering "The Saints Go Marching In" badly accompanied by a guitar in discord. The waiter walks in, starts to pass Joe's table. He notices people offstage noticing Sandra.)

WAITER: Hey! That the same chick you was with? *(Joe, preoccupied, nods, goes to the wall telephone.)* How come she's always cutting out? *(pause, Joe dialing)* — If she was *my* woman I'd take her home and give her what she's looking for —

JOE: *(waves him aside)* Harold? Dwayne. *(pause)* The boat? We

87

THE PLIGHT OF THE LESSER SAWYER'S CRICKET

changed our minds. Thanks, anyway . . . *(pause)* What's wrong with my voice! Did you ever hear of such a thing as air pollution? *(pause)* Listen — I'm taking my kids on an ecological expedition . . . *(pause) Ecological* . . . Yeah . . . we were supposed to go Wednesday, but I just found out it's been changed. Could you tell my wife — *(pause)* Oh, never mind. I'm confused about the date . . . *(pause) Date!* as in calendar . . . *(pause)* Yeah . . . Listen — do you know anything about the Hooton Dam? *(pause)* I didn't think so — It's about time people learned what's going on around there . . . *(pause)* The Hooton Dam project is going to fuck up the crickets, that's all . . . *(pause) Cricket!* Those bugs that chirp in the night . . . *(pause) Drinking!* In this place?! Listen, the Lesser Sawyer Cricket needs all the help . . .

(Harold has hung up. Joe stares at the mouthpiece, then slowly replaces it.)

CURTAIN

CONDITIONED REFLEX

A One-Act Satire Tragedy in Verse

CHARACTERS:

The Analyst
The Patient

THE TIME:

The Late 1960's

THE PLACE:

A psychiatrist's suite eleven floors above the streets of an urban area.

CONDITIONED RELFEX

NOTES ON THE CHARACTERS:

THE ANALYST

A rather conventional middle-class man; he is of course disciplined, conservative, logical, and tends to understate. In situations where the patient baits him or contrives annoying acts, the analyst will meet them with his trademarked, conditioned reflexes. There will occur times when his irritation or contempt show through, but he will quickly recover. His only catharsis occurs when he is faced by the patient's knife—for, realistically, he will recognize the danger he is in. From then on he will fight for control—to play out his proper role despite the fact that the patient will be in the driver's seat. Also, there will be certain visible "ticks" on the part of the analyst—blowing his nose, coughing, clearing throat, etc.

THE PATIENT

An extremely complex individual. His emotions range from anger to likable charm. In between, he will occasionally break into real laughter, he will whisper and mildly rant. In his poetic soliloquies his diction will be Shakespearean—an actor glorying in the role. But he will change pace constantly, going from clipped, flip remarks or accusations to pleadings and cold anger.

As to appearance; the analyst will of course wear a suit and tie. The patient is very casual—growth of beard, sweatshirt, running shoes, jeans—or, in effect, the rich, casual, idle, arrogant scion who doesn't have to conform.

AT RISE

The stage is dark. We see only the face of the patient rather impressively lighted.

PATIENT: *(as a poetic, dramatic reading; slow, eloquent)*
    It was an owl's night
      For the invented moons.
    And yarded dogs, barking by the hundreds
    Seemed to sense
    The unfenced
      Facelessness of me —
    Each with his dream of unarmed robbers . . .

(The patient plants a cigarette between his lips. It remains there unlighted. The stage spots come up now to reveal the couch upon which he rests, and also the desk at which the analyst sits, taking notes.)

    (in a more down-to-earth voice)
    And I stood there, the while, listening,
      While the sea waited and wetted, and
    Wept wonderingly.
        With seven million dollars in my pocket! Plus
    A piece of paper
    Containing the forged signatures
    Of members of the board —
    Confession to a crime
    I'd never dare commit.
    Meanwhile, I got out the piece of rope I'd hidden away.

    (almost joyously)
    Got a light Doctor?

(The analyst either reaches over and hands him his gold lighter or arises from his chair and lights the patient's cigarette.)

ANALYST: *(in the cool, emotionless voice usually employed)*
    And then what happened?

PATIENT: Nothing. It always does.

CONDITIONED REFLEX

ANALYST: *(unrebuffed, ignoring the patient's little victory. He half turns in his chair and his voice will be imploring, clinical, persisting.)* When you think of "nothing," what comes to mind?

PATIENT: Nothing, Doctor.

(He lets this sink in, then props himself up on his elbows.)

    So I'm resisting —
    But resisting *creatively,* wouldn't you say?

(He waits, but the analyst is dead still.)

    But as you say
    It's *my* money. And
    My problem. So —

(Deliberately he reaches over the couch and mashes the cigarette out on the carpet.)

    I'll give it to you.
    I took out the rope and tied up the yacht.

(Unobtrusively the analyst gets up and places an ashtray next to the patient.)

    Yachts remind me of chauffeurs
    And this reminds me
      I forgot to tell you
    I remembered to forget my rubbers.
(Reproachfully, he pauses to recognize the ashtray.)

    I dismissed the chauffeur and
      Started to walk — the weather on that occasion
    Seemed to suit my mood —
      Thunder and lightning . . .
    And, I believe, a typhoon.
      They don't make them that way anymore, Doctor,
      — the nights —

(in a hurried whisper)
Somewhere
A mockingbird sang The Star-Spangled Banner
And I —

CONDITIONED RELFEX

>There by appointment to absolutely no one
>Heard 'gainst that throttled dark
>The arresting cry of sirens . . .
>>Strictly routine —
>
>Another crazy man was on the town!
>The fox was on the hounds.

ANALYST: So, what about foxes?

PATIENT: Like a fox I'm crazy!
>I identify
>>With the hunter and hunted. I
>
>Smell the vaportrails of men engaged
>In a violation of men. While the
>>Silent overshoes of prowlcars park
>>>In public parks
>>
>>Among the people who park
>>>In parked cars with people
>>
>For those things which
>>Are the park's
>>For parking.

ANALYST: *(after a pause; almost with a sigh)* What comes to mind when you think of parks?

PATIENT: Horses—
>Parks remind me of horses
>And horses bring up John Wayne
>>Riding hard!
>>Scowling and dangerous!
>>And shooting straight as he rides!

ANALYST: Anything else?

PATIENT: His is the arm of right and might, Doctor.
>Every girl leans toward his
>>Great pounding heart.
>
>He is Father — husband — lover —
>>And the rest of us sit by and watch;
>
>God made a great mistake when he invented the
>Majority of men . . .

CONDITIONED REFLEX

ANALYST: *(quickly, to catch the patient offguard)*
    What *about* girls?

PATIENT: When I think about girls I keep getting boys.

ANALYST: All right. What about boys?

PATIENT: *(capriciously)*
    Boys only bring up girls again.

(The analyst coughs, clears his throat.)

    (now with rebuke)
    Your cough, Doctor — it tells me all
      You're not going to say.
    — Poor little rich bastard with his nightclubs
    And swimming pools
    And his gifted dodge of dialogue!
      He knows all your answers, but
      Can't solve his problems . . .

ANALYST: *(exploringly, as though ignoring the last)*
    Let's try going back to parks. What comes to mind?

PATIENT: *Baseball.*
    But John Wayne's in it again *(with anger)*
    He's winding up for the pitch
    And the Bosox just walked home.
      See that
    Winning scowl! Wayne's
      Angry and American!
      Nobody else will make it home . . .
    Got a light?

(The analyst hands him the lighter.)

    (igniting cigarette, hands it back)
    Home reminds me of a seaside house
      I see *me* now —
      No one else did! *(his voice trailing off confidingly)*
    No one knows —
    But *I* know that I

> *Knew!*
>
> *(suddenly solicitous)*
> Am I telling you anything you want to know?

ANALYST: Well, what do you think?

PATIENT: *(in an unexpected burst)*
> I hated my father! mother! sister! brother!
> Uncles and aunts!

(The analyst clears his throat.)

> *(the patient acting as though he heard the sound)*
> Yes!
> I must be on the right track. Yes —
> Brilliant family.
>   Lawyers and counts,
>   Engineers and actresses
> With in-laws and outlaws
> After the great tradition.
> *(abusively)*
> But they took away my special driver's license
> When I was twelve
> And pulled me out of Andover for hazing
> I broke three legs on five horses that season —
> And my father refused me the use of the yacht —
> *(his voice trailing off)*
> After I ran it aground one stinking,
>   Drinking, wet night.

(He leans over, places the ashtray on his belly, but crushes the cigarette on the carpet again.)

> *(in a burst of self-discovery)*
> I keep doing things
> That make people want to punish me!

ANALYST: Why do you think you wished to be punished?

PATIENT: Because I stole my brother's movie camera.

ANALYST: All right, you stole your brother's camera. What does that

CONDITIONED REFLEX

              remind you of?

PATIENT: Bentley. *(a pause of finality)*

ANALYST: And what about Mr. Bentley?

PATIENT: *(impatiently, yet triumphantly)*
              Bentley *car.* Automobile!
              I stole my brother's Bentley . . . and
              (now poetically)
              Drove straight to the heart of the full moon.
                 There were crickets and foxes
              Ejaculating incessantly
              In a night hot with hay. But I wasn't lonely,
              Doctor.
                 I also stole my brother's girl friend.

ANALYST: *Now* do you think of boys when you recall girls?

PATIENT: No. Just now
              When I think of girls, I get
                 Little girls.

ANALYST: So —?

PATIENT: So it has something to do with that, doesn't it?

(He waits, but the analyst is silent and still. Impulsively he gets up from the couch and takes a couple of steps toward the window.)

              (in a halted but poetic rendering)
              I tried to drown my stepsister's child
                 In the swimming pool —
              The butler saw me, and
                 Was asked to resign.
              My father paid my tuition
                 Into and out of
              Schools, jails, scrapes and lawsuits.
              But our neighbors were wealthy; not for sale,
              They reported me to the Humane Society, and
              (lowering his voice)
              For reasons I am unable to recall . . .

CONDITIONED RELFEX

> My dog was taken away.

(He leans on the windowsill; the analyst rises.)

> What is the difference between normal and abnormal?
> I demanded only a fulfillment
>   of the basic urges!
> My father bought me what he could, but
>   He couldn't
> Afford to give me what I wanted.
> Yet,
> *(facing the analyst)*
> All I wanted was my normal share
> Of the good things of life.

(The analyst comes to the window as though unobtrusively to herd the patient back to his couch.)

> Is that so abnormal, Doctor?

ANALYST: Let us, for a moment, think about abnormality.
   It is normal
   To wish to be a man among men
     As well as
   Women.

(The analyst subtly backs the patient toward the couch.)

PATIENT: I don't want sympathy, Doctor.

ANALYST: *(taking more steps toward the couch)*
   *Understand*ing!
     It is quite natural you'd envy your
     Brother his success
      While at the same time, be jealous
     Of sister.

PATIENT: I dont want *understand*ing, Doctor

ANALYST: You were an average sibling
   In a brilliant family —

(The analyst stops before the cigarettes on the carpet and bends to pick

CONDITIONED REFLEX

them up.)

          Hostilities
          Under the circumstances —

(At this time the patient brushes against the desk. We see him pick up and pocket the analyst's gold lighter.)

PATIENT: *(whirls around, interrupting)*
          But to *steal*, Doctor —!

ANALYST: Most of us would steal our
          "brother's automobile"
          Were it not for the fear
          Of being punished.

PATIENT: *(Somewhat soothed, he again takes his position on the couch.)*
          But I set fire to my sister's dress!

ANALYST: Sister was unable to return your love.

PATIENT: There was that which I planned to do to my father
          One rainy, dark night . . .

ANALYST: *(sitting at his desk once again. He doesn't notice the lighter's absence.)*
          Father refused to let you use the boat.

PATIENT: What about mother —?
          I accused her of having an affair
          — with a psychiatrist.

ANALYST: *(doesn't rise to the thrust)*
          Mother
          Like sister —
          Was prevented by custom
          From returning your love.

PATIENT: You are able to turn it around
             To sound . . . so
          Understandable!
          So normal!

ANALYST: *(as he puts a cigarette in his mouth)*

The *desire* is normal —
You were the black sheep!
The member of the team
Who lowered the family batting average.
The abnormality —

(He looks for the lighter; starts to reach into his pockets.)

If there be one —
Is that your fantasies haven't taken the form
Of a Death-Wish.

PATIENT: *(leans around on an elbow to face the analyst. The analyst ceases his search for the lighter.)*
How do you know they haven't?

ANALYST: *(removes cigarette, places it back in his cigarette case)*
I don't think it likely you'd be here
Today
If you had.

PATIENT: No, Doctor?

ANALYST: *(again starts feeling his pockets for the lighter)*
(with a slightest show of irritation)
Oh, no doubt in your wishful fantasies
You did away with father and brother —
(emits a short, curled laugh)
Perhaps even slept incestuously with mother
And sister!
(He gets control of his hands and relaxes.)
But you didn't carry them out!
You had too much to lose!

PATIENT: *What* did I have to lose!

ANALYST: *(with a shrug)*
Money.
Position.
Champagne, girls, cars, boats —
The freedom to go about pretty much as
you please —

CONDITIONED REFLEX

                The scion of a family of position
                (a leer in his voice now)
                Used to pushing people out of his way.
                Death or imprisonment
                Would be quite another thing —

PATIENT: Congratulate me, Doctor!
            I've finally gotten you to say it!

(The analyst absently gets out his cigarette case again and puts a cigarette between his lips. He glances for the lighter, takes out the cigarette and speaks.)

ANALYST: *(in an apologetic explanation)*
            I may have said too much. If so, in the main,
            I was trying to point up the realistic reasons
            Which work on your side.

(The analyst again feels through his pockets.)

PATIENT: Nevertheless, I'm a sick man, Doctor. Even
            My *appearance* suggests it; I'll
            Never be like others —

ANALYST: *(puts the cigarette back into his case)*
            Perhaps you don't have to be.
            A man with a yacht is rarely
            Dangerous.
            (He sits back in the chair.)
            Now — what *about* sickness?
            What comes to *mind?*

PATIENT: My brother. He was healthy.

ANALYST: All right. What do you see?

PATIENT: A cemetery.

ANALYST: And "cemetery" brings up what?

PATIENT: Graves.
            My mother
            My father
            My sister —

ANALYST: Go on —

PATIENT: That's all.

ANALYST: *(significantly)* No brother?

(The patient remains silent. Deliberately he plants a cigarette in his mouth and brings forth the analyst's gold lighter. He lights up. The analyst is writing. He smells the smoke; he also gets out a cigarette and then remembers he has no lighter.)

PATIENT: *(in a quiet, new voice)*
I see John Wayne now.

(The analyst clears his throat.)

He's going to beat hell out of me. Why?

ANALYST: Well, why do you think?

PATIENT: Because I'm a spoiled, soft
Hothouse flower;
Unable to take my place among American men
Who are men
Among men
Or women —
Or men —

(The patient lights up again. He steps over to the analyst and lights his cigarette for him. The analyst watches in a vague fascination, the sight of his own lighter.)

(beginning to raise his voice)
I plucked the wings off my
Brother's model airplane, Doctor;
Then,
Rather than face the consequences,
Hid in the maid's bathroom.

(He strolls toward the window once more.)

I lied
When my father asked me who stole his liquor.
I bought myself a few friends,

CONDITIONED REFLEX

        Then,
      Bribed them to supply me with drugs, narcotics;
        And when
      I tortured some kid half my size —
      Convinced the juvenile officer
      I'd been attacked with a knife.
      While the others played baseball
      I practiced deceit.
      Strangers thought I was gentle and good and
                        ..... *Misunderstood* —
    (in a roar)
      Doctor! I'd just as leave kill everybody as not!

ANALYST: *(unimpressed, clinical, probing)*
      When you think of killing
        Who comes to mind?

PATIENT: *(starts toward the analyst)*
      You.

(The analyst puts a hand to his mouth as though to suggest he is bored to the point of yawning. But he dutifully jots notes, not glancing up at the patient.)

      Yes — put that in writing, too!
        You —
      With your castrating semantics
        Superimposing upon me your charts of
          human behavior
        And peering through the unmatched holes through me!
      Round me! Inside my rusted
          mental machinery!
        — So
        Go
          Ahead, and taste corrosion; Smell
      My unlit gasses
        At a hundred bucks an hour!

(Abruptly he turns his back and starts toward the window.)

      I've an artificial brain, and

        A glass eye, Doctor
        But I feel you through the back of my head —
        Fighting contempt,
        Wrestling your own self-righteousness
          Listening for the lips of some
            Sociological cipher
              While ever so faintly —
        Your disdain shows!

(The patient places his hands on the windowsill again; with less anger, with more prophecy, he continues.)

        But you'll go on
          Picking up the pieces
          Trying to save something from this dwarfed psyche
        Labeling it all
          Neat and understandable to suit your science!
          But you can't recognize me, Doctor!
          I'm not you!

(The analyst gets up and starts toward the window.)

ANALYST: So, who do you *really* want to kill —?

PATIENT: You.
               I resent your personal success. And
           Your right to practice.
               How can you know disease
               When you've never been sick!

(The analyst comes alongside him now, with another unlit cigarette between his lips.)

               Don't come too near me!
               You might catch it!

ANALYST: *(stepping back)*
        — Got a light?

(The patient pulls out the lighter. He lights the analyst's cigarette, accepting one for himself. He lights his own, then waves it as though extinguishing a match, and tosses it out the window.)

CONDITIONED REFLEX

PATIENT: Look down there, Doctor —

(The analyst steps forward and looks.)

    How many stories is it — a dozen?
    That's your story. That's how far
      You are
        From reality.
    And I'm way out there, too,
      In left field
      My back to the ball;
    A fragment of the cloistered dissonance
      Where psychopaths spring like toadstools
      From a park's murky shadows —
    Waiting to test their unconditioned reflexes
    'Gainst careless people
      Who no longer care!

(He moves away from the window, toward the analysts's desk.)

    There's your story, Doctor!
    A million bodies
      Decaying
    From the inside out!
    . . . . . And only you
      To defend the Norm
        Against them!

(At the couch he turns and faces the analyst.)

    We outnumber you, sir!
    You'd better work fast!

ANALYST: *(standing straight beside his chair)*
    So you're no longer in a minority — *(He sits down.)*

PATIENT: *(sits on the couch; humorously)*
    I lay claim to certain unique behaviorisms.
    (He settles back, folds his arms.)
    I tried to set an old man onto my sister
      When she was eleven . . .

CONDITIONED RELFEX

ANALYST: *(baiting the patient now. Now that the crisis has been weathered he can be more forceful.)*
You want me to hate you! Don't hold back!
Give me something to hate!

PATIENT: I propositioned my mother when *I* was eleven.

ANALYST: It is understandable that the son —

PATIENT: *(cuts him off)*
I know! You told me! *(Loftily he adds:)*
I also tried to poison my father on his
sixty-third birthday.

ANALYST: The father-figure is traditionally —

PATIENT: *(cutting him off)*
I know! You told me!

ANALYST: *(with tolerance showing through)*
So what about "being told?"

PATIENT: Everything fed into your
Psychological IBM machine comes out
Cautiously set
In grey type. Doctor —
Cold-blooded murder would
Melt in your mouth!
If I "told you" I'd shot the vice president
Of the United States
You'd understand
Before you heard!

(He sits up in an emulation of the analyst and mimics him in voice.)

"*Naturally,* you killed the vice president!
Everybody wants to —
A man among men! Formidable rival and
Symbol of sex!
It is quite understandable — so
Perfectly normal —
This desire to eliminate the Father-figure!"

CONDITIONED REFLEX

ANALYST: *(chidingly)*
    So you're not so especially unusual after all . . .

PATIENT: *(deathly still now. In a sly, pregnant voice:)*
    But there *is* something unusual about me, Doctor.

ANALYST: *(writing notes)* What comes to mind?

PATIENT: A woman's wrist watch.

ANALYST: *(patronizingly)* All right, what about a woman's wrist watch?

PATIENT: It was lying on your receptionist's desk as I walked past.

(We see the analyst stiffen but the patient cannot. The analyst's voice seems to be utterly detatched.)

ANALYST: Well? So —

PATIENT: Doesn't that make me pretty low?
    Stealing from the people who're
    Trying to help solve my problem?

ANALYST: Do you want to feel "low?"

PATIENT: Yes! No! I don't know —
    Aren't you going to tell *her* where it is? She's
    Probably worried.

ANALYST: That's *her* problem.

PATIENT: She's quite attractive. And
    Seemed so —
        Illogical
        Inferior —
        Attainable —

ANALYST: That's *your* problem.

PATIENT: So I would do that to her
    So I'm sick
    (in a crazy whisper)
    But it's perfectly okay
    Because we understand *why* —

CONDITIONED RELFEX

(The analyst blows his nose.)

PATIENT: Doctor — did you know I was going to
Jump out of that window?

ANALYST: But you didn't.

PATIENT: How were you sure I wouldn't?
(He holds up his hands.)
Wait! I know!
A self-punishment wish is one thing —
To carry it out is another!
The line between sanity and insanity
Is the difference between
Reality and wishful-thinking.
Shall I go on?

(The analyst remains fixed and silent.)

The insane man punishes himself
The normal
Takes it out on some acceptable hate-object
Like the vice president. Or
— If you object to the simile —
Substitute yourself.

ANALYST: *(playing along with it)* Therefore —

PATIENT: How are you going to prevent me
From committing an immoral act?

ANALYST: Science is not concerned with "moral"
And "immoral,"
We have been through this —

PATIENT: *(He blows his nose.)* We've been through everything, Doctor.

ANALYST: We can teach you only
How to drive your own machine.
How you drive it —

PATIENT: Is my problem.

CONDITIONED REFLEX

                But what if I drive it into my analyst's
                Cadillac?

ANALYST: What happens to the analyst's Cadillac is his problem
                What happens to you —
                Should you do this —
                (He shrugs.)
                Arrest . . . perhaps jail . . . perhaps suspension of
                    Operator's license . . . and
                    Damage to your own machine.

PATIENT: Suppose I've
                Already had my license suspended;
                Suppose, perhaps
                My machine's
                    An old '38 Chevy
                And to me jail's
                No worse than other forms of imprisonment?
                I'm a sick man, Doctor.
                I warn you of intentions
                  But all I get
                  Is something like,
                "What comes to mind when you think of 'intentions?' "
                All right! *(He sits up.)*
                I *intend* to take your cigarette case.
                (He reaches over and does so.)

ANALYST: All right. Why?
                At fifteen dollars apiece you could afford
                A thousand.

PATIENT: *(holding up his hand)*
                Not only do I take it! But also
                  I know *why!*

ANALYST: Well, why —?

PATIENT: To punish you? Sure, but
                Also
                  Because it is valuable. I —
                      Want it!

CONDITIONED RELFEX

ANALYST: Suppose I also want it.

PATIENT: You can rationalize your wants —
    Condition them —
    Accept reality —

ANALYST: *(in his exploring voice which disregards past subject matter)*
What comes to mind when you think of Reality?

PATIENT: Reality is not quite good enough for some of us, Doctor.
    We come to your for help
    And you get out your conformist cages
        And talk us in;
Predicting tomorrow,
Explaining today,
And putting the blame on yesterday.
(with renewed vigor)
But how do you *know* what you know.
    About us? — you weren't there!
Have you felt the shiver of cheap hotels
And stood in line for
    Soup and songs?
Have you ever begged for a pint of wine while
    A prostitute spit in your cup?
Have you come apart publicly
And had your pieces
    Picked up for
For vagrancy?
(with frightening laughter)
You understand statistics —
But you'd better give me
    What I've come for!
You might yourself become a statistic!

ANALYST: *(thinks for a moment; then, as though ignoring all of the patient's tirade:)*
— What comes to you *now*
    When I mention your father's yacht?

CONDITIONED REFLEX

PATIENT: There wasn't any goddamned yacht.

ANALYST: *(again ignoring the patient's statement, with a voice new and exploring)* For a moment, let's think about your brother's car. — A Jaguar, wasn't it?

PATIENT: He didn't have a car.
I didn't have a brother

(The analyst starts to fish for his cigarette case; then he remembers. He makes a shrugging gesture.)

ANALYST: — Gone.

PATIENT: Gone — father, sister, mother, brother.
All of them.
(brutally)
Fantasies, Doctor!

ANALYST: *(somewhat shaken but remaining the clinician)*
And likewise, the "inferiority complex —?"

PATIENT: It *wasn't* a complex. I *am* inferior.
— And these are the only clothes I have.

ANALYST: *(breaks his pencil)* Anything else concerning "fantasies?"

PATIENT: My bank account.
The Beverly Hills address.
I live off Main Street.
Skid row, Doctor!
On an unlisted alley . . .

ANALYST: What *about* "bank account."

PATIENT: Good free-association, Doctor!
How can I afford analysis
If I've no bank account?

(He holds up his hands as though stretching an object between them.)

Rubber checks.
They'll snap back in a week or so.

            (thoughtfully)
            Where'll *I* be in a week or so? Vegas?
              Mexico?
            Or will my dreams stay inside a bottle of Muscatel.

ANALYST: *(getting the picture and not liking it. He exhibits various nervous reactions, but in voice he continues to remain detached and explorative.)*
            Let us continue with fantasies.
            (brightly)
            Fantasies often are quite revealing.
            Do other fantasies come to mind?

PATIENT: *(semi-poetically as in the beginning)*
            The house beside the sea
              And the yarded dogs, an owl's moon . . .
            The unfenced facelessness of me . . . retread,
              Of the anonymous man!
            Unwanted
              But wanting-in. Why? What do I see inside?
            There — on the marble table!
              What do I see, Doctor?

ANALYST: *(quickly, relievedly)* Yes! What do you see?

PATIENT: A million dollars in paper and currency.

ANALYST: *(in the saddle now)* Anything else?

PATIENT: Seven cents.
            Nickel, and two pennies.

ANALYST: What else do you see in the picture?

PATIENT: Foxes!
             Scowling faces —
            Superimposed upon one another. And
            All of them staring over my shoulder.
            All of them wanting that money.
              Who are they, Doctor?

ANALYST: Well, who do you think?

CONDITIONED REFLEX

PATIENT: My father, my mother,
My sister and brother —
— Cigarette?

(He reaches out over his shoulder holding out the case. The analyst accepts it.)

ANALYST: A light, please?

(The patient hands over the lighter.)

(lighting up, enjoying it)
So everything returns —
Comes back —

PATIENT: Not really —
Only as wishful-thinking.
— May *I* have a cigarette, Doctor?

(The analyst hands him back the case.)

And a light.

(The analyst gives him the lighter.)

(after lighting up—and placing both objects back in his pocket)
I see John Wayne now
And a famous politician —
Who, I don't know —
The name escapes me.
Suddenly — *(He sits bolt upright.)*
All of us race toward that table!
(He gets up, reeling slightly.)
My legs are of rubber!
They're sticking to my hands! And
My hands!
They're glued to my pockets!

(He drags toward the window. The analyst gets up.)

There's a scuffle! Angry voices and thunderbolts!
But I'm filled with power!
With a superhuman thrust my right hand

Comes free!
Doctor! I hear a shot!
Do you hear it!

(The analyst moves rapidly toward the window. The patient sags as though purged, against the sill. The analyst stands a polite distance behind the patient's back.)

(sad, contrite)
They're all watching me now;
Faces shocked, angry, accusing. John Wayne —
Two pistols 'round his massive thighs
And those ready hands
At his own hips!
— I have done it, he says!
But what! What! What!

ANALYST: *(blurting it out, afraid of he knows not what)*
Yes! What!

PATIENT: *(whirling around in a snarl, a switchblade knife in his right hand)*
I shot the vice president of the United States!

(The analyst retreats toward the couch, backing up. The patient follows, driving him.)

(There follows an awkward pause. Both seem to listen for outside sounds but there are none. The analyst is playing it cool. He is aware of his dangerous situation, but his emotions are conditioned.)

(in a quiet, mocking voice)
And then what happened, Doctor?

ANALYST: *(taking two more backward steps, the patient following)* The patient tired of the fantasy— *(haltingly)* He wanted a real death.

PATIENT: With a real weapon. *(With the knife he waves the analyst to the couch.)*
— Doctor?

(The analyst obeys. The patient indicates he wants him to lie down. The

CONDITIONED REFLEX

    analyst objects but he knows that the man must be humored.)
        Yes.
        Try to relax.
        Let your thoughts go . . .

ANALYST: *(halfway between clinical and man-to-man)*
        What do you *think* you want from me?

PATIENT: *(stands by the desk. His voice is mocking.)*
        What I *think* I want
        Is your life.

(The analyst goes through the motions of seeking his cigarette case again. The patient lets him take one from the case, lights it for him.)
        Unbutton your coat. Loosen your necktie.
        Let everything go . . .
        (He waits, the analyst stays groomed.)
        . . . . . Your *way* of life, Doctor!
        Not your disfigured body!
        I covet your cars! servants! horses! Your
        Beautiful rich, sick women.
        The *Scene* —
           But that's not all!
        I covet your distinguished appearance. Your
           Education and orientation
           I want to be a man among men and
           A man among women!
        (almost appealingly)
        Doctor!
         I want to be *you!*
         Not me!
         (He slumps into the analyst's chair.)

ANALYST: I am not God.
        I can do nothing
        About that.

PATIENT: *(menacingly now)*
        It's too bad, Doctor!

I'm a hungry man, Doctor!

ANALYST: *(doggedly and without hope)* I can only help you to drive your own machine —

PATIENT: *(abusively)*
We've done that bit! I *am*
Driving it!
— Fast! Reckless! Dangerously!
I've nothing to lose!

ANALYST: Your *life,* perhaps —
Your freedom of movement.
The odds are against the lawbreaker —

PATIENT: *(cutting him off)*
You think you can rationalize my hostility?
Don't try!
I resent your logic!
Reason is my lifelong enemy.

(He picks up the analyst's pad and pencil as though about to become clinical; then begins anew in the analyst's tone of voice.)

— Doctor, what comes to mind when you think of "life?"

ANALYST: Time.

PATIENT: And, time?

ANALYST: *(brings out his watch and glances at it)* I have an appointment in seven minutes.

(The patient brings forth the woman's wrist watch. He glances at it, then lays it on the table.)

PATIENT: We should synchronize our watches.
I have considerably more time than that.

(He raises up, reaches over and holds out his hand for the analyst's watch. The analyst yields it.)

(thoughtfully. He places both watches on the desk.)
— What *about* time and life?

CONDITIONED REFLEX

ANALYST: Life brings up disappointments.

PATIENT: So what about disappointments?

ANALYST: Some of my patients have failed to respond to treatment.

PATIENT: *(boredly, after the manner)* Anything else?

ANALYST: *(falling into his reverse role now)*
    Patients remind me of hospitals
    And hospitals bring up a child
        With tight, mincing lips.
        His father is dead, and
    He is stealing an apple from a blind woman.
        Not for hunger!
        For practice!
    Later he was to graduate from N.Y.U.

PATIENT: *(holding the pad and pencil in a clinical manner)*
    Does that suggest anything to you?

ANALYST: Obviously,
    The boy was compensating for his unfortunate childhood.
        He would become a Doctor
        A psychiatrist
    And devote his life to Finding Out
    About Finding Out
        About Finding Out.

(The patient coughs, says nothing.)

        I see mother now!
        I brought her an apple —
        (His voice trails off.)
        She was blind —
        To my faults.

PATIENT: *(sternly)* You're resisting —

ANALYST: I have nothing to hide.

PATIENT: *Hide!*
    What comes to you

CONDITIONED RELFEX

	When you think of "hide?"
ANALYST:	Seek!
PATIENT:	And *seek?*
ANALYST:	Hide and seek Cat and mouse.
PATIENT:	What else about "seek?"
ANALYST:	Seek and ye shall find.
PATIENT:	— And where is it hidden —?
ANALYST:	*(blurting it out against his wishes)* What — My *wallet?*
PATIENT:	*(after a pause)* What about — Wallet?
ANALYST:	It is in my overcoat pocket
PATIENT:	*(from the desk he glances quickly around the room)* — And the overcoat?
ANALYST:	I — *(He raises up on his elbows and also looks around.)* I have forgotten where I placed it.
PATIENT:	*(sternly)* One *doesn't forget!*

(The patient jumps up and stands looking down at the analyst. He sees that the latter needs a light. He attends to his cigarette. The analyst, we see, looks covetously at the lighter.)

ANALYST:	I'd appreciate it if you'd let me keep the lighter. It's a class trophy — a prize For scholarship —
PATIENT:	*(squinting at the engraving on the lighter for the first time. Then, in an accusing voice:)* — That's not your name, Doctor!
ANALYST:	No. It wasn't a functional name — For psychological reasons

CONDITIONED REFLEX

                I had it changed.

PATIENT: *(dryly)*
                And I, also. Often —
                    For *functional* reasons —

ANALYST: I *came* from your world —
                I am only a convenient symbol for your hostilities.
                — Anyone could have played the role.

PATIENT: But who better
                Than analyst and patient can
                    Exchange roles?
                (in his mock-clinical voice)
                What comes to mind when you think of "roles?"

ANALYST: Butter.
                We used oleo on our bread;
                I grew up on the East Side.
                The girl next door married
                The boy across the street . . .

PATIENT: *(dryly, having lost his pseudo-analytical style)*
                You're killing me, Doctor.

ANALYST: During summer vacations
                I cleaned cesspools
                    To support my mother
                Who worked as a waitress.

PATIENT: *(not to be outdone)*
                My father was a bookie. He bet
                Everything he had
                    On a *saloon* waitress.

ANALYST: *(continuing in the same vein)*
                My family was unlisted
                    In city directories
                        For four generations back.

PATIENT: We festered in the same swamp, Doctor
                Both gravitating

CONDITIONED RELFEX

> From nothing to something.
> But you turned right;
> — and I —

(He goes over to the desk and picks up the watch, glances at it. He picks up the knife.)

> *(in a whisper)*
> Doctor —
> For once in my life —
> For a fraction of the fifty-minute hour
> I'm having my moment!
> We're equals!

ANALYST: *(summing it up)*
Position and wealth
Versus failure
And a knife.

PATIENT: The analyst's couch
Or the electric chair —
Which'll it be?
What do you think about your overcoat *now*,
Doctor?

ANALYST: *(having made a decision)*
Suddenly it comes back to me!
I didn't wear an overcoat this morning
The morning
Started out
A fine day!

PATIENT: *(prodding)* — Therefore?

ANALYST: *(reaching into his pocket)*
Therefore, it must be — *(brings forth the wallet)*
Yes!

(The patient arises, steps over to the couch and the analyst hands him the wallet.)

PATIENT: Goodbye, Doctor —

121

CONDITIONED REFLEX

(The analyst slowly gets up. He straightens his hair, tie, etc.)

ANALYST: *(part facetiously, part gratefully)*
— That's all for today — ?

CURTAIN

ALTERNATE ENDING

PATIENT: Goodbye, Doctor —

(The analyst slowly gets up. He straightens his hair, tie, etc.)

ANALYST: *(part facetiously, part gratefully)*
— That's all for today — ?

PATIENT: That's all I'm not so sick as I was—

(As though by unconscious agreement now they trade roles. The analyst now stands at his desk, arranging things, getting ready for the next customer. Now the patient tosses the lighter to the desk.)

Here's your prize—

ANALYST: *(with businesslike smile)*
Keep it. You won.

PATIENT: *(He starts to pick it up, then doesn't.)*
No. Doctor. *You*—
You relieved my hostilities.

(He examines the wallet, then grandly peels off two tens and a five. He lets them float to the floor. He pockets the rest and tosses the wallet back.)

You can *keep your identity*—
Diner's Club card, country club pass—
Operator's license which permits you
to *drive* your own *machine*—

(The desk buzzer rings. The analyst glances at the patient. The patient nods.)

CONDITIONED RELFEX

The analyst goes to desk and cuts off buzzer. The patient waits.)

ANALYST: *(formally)* Same time next week?

PATIENT: Oh! I had meant to discuss that with you, Doctor.

(He glances toward receptionist's door, then at door through which he will exit.)

>Obviously,
>>I've reached a point where I'm able to
>>Solve my own problems,
>>Handle my hostilities
>>>In my own way.
>
>*(brightly)*
>
>I think the analysis could end *now!*

ANALYST: *(now curtly; in a wry voice)*
>Realistically speaking
>>For the patient to continue
>>>Would be a waste of time and money.
>
>*(pause)*
>>—He's—

PATIENT: *(The buzzer rings again. He goes quickly to the exit door and stops.)*
>Yes, Doctor!
>>He's—
>Gone just about as far as he can go.

CURTAIN

Curtis Zahn

STORIES

THE ABSOLUTELY NAKED TRUTH ABOUT MY PROBLEM

Complete strangers approach me at all times with their threadbare pretensions of collective hope.

By this, I mean to say that I exude some extraordinary magnetism over which I have small control. They come with their great loneliness, seeing in me the ally; a person to take their side in any argument against civilization. I have, they surmise, an intelligence superior to theirs—I am their reward for a life-long search. They see me and know . . .

"Your ego is insufferable, " some will say, when and if they come to know me better (but few do), then add, "the more I see of you, the less I think of you. In fact, at this moment you are despicable. "

Regrettably, this affects me little. I suggest to them that they can always seek out another God, guru, hero or mentor, or whatever it is they are looking for. I've my own clientele. For everyone who goes away, disillusioned, hordes are waiting. This is true; I've only to walk down a public street to pick up a multitude or two. Some are, of course shy or proud, and must devise some excuse for meeting me. For example, in a cafe, a stranger at a nearby table will drop his plate, get up and say, "Pardon me—, " then promptly introduce himself. Or, if I am on a deserted beach, someone will come straight from nowhere and ask if I saw a small, grey, lost dog. Because I despise subterfuge I am apt to reply, "Yes — I did see a small, grey dog. But I didn't ask if it was lost. I mind my own business. " The stranger, rebuffed, knows he should leave. But he cannot, of course, because of this confounded magnetism I have. He will discover himself to be out of matches, or out of cigarettes. Being the kind of person I am—generous to a fault, although intolerant of contrived excuses—I offer him either or both. The stranger—overcome with gratitude—will ask if I voted democrat or republican. Sometimes I cannot remember, even for people who succeeded in getting to know me. Politely I answer that I am scheduled to make a public appearance at three-thirty and hurry away, my head bowed in concentration. I often concentrate when not otherwise busy at thinking creatively. When I do have time to think, I usually think about myself—

127

for lack of comparatively worthy subject matter. Yet, I have not really solved the problem—which is that I am a natural leader, desperately trying to evade history.

"You're a pompous ass!" one of my many girlfriends told me on a night when it rained, and the street crowds could overhear, and a Greyhound bus was waiting alongside us while its passengers vainly tried to get their damn windows open in order to see me. "I agree, " I told her, "but the people never learn. " Just then the driver stepped down, came over, and began to plead for my autograph. "How shall I sign it?" I asked tolerantly, "I mean, what name?"

"Any name! Names don't matter—it's the person that counts!"

This more or less illustrates my complaint. (The girl, incidentally, disappeared into the crowd—drenched in her own humility.) For example, when people gather around an automobile accident, or a fight between a cop and a demonstrator, someone near me will announce, loudly, "That's a hell of a thing, isn't it?" and then try to engage me in a conversation about yachts or electronics. On trains, women who are as old as I, but have daughters who think and feel as I do, will affix me with a frank, conspiratorial smile. As though to say, "Nice to have you aboard—you're the first interesting person I've met in a long time, and this is my fourteenth trip around the world. "

"We haven't met!" I remind her, or them. It sounds callous. I really am not. But there simply is only so much of me to spread so thinly over so many. In public parks (where I am careful not to go, except between midnight and dawn) wild-eyed men with Bibles spring at me with the truth—even though they suspect I already have it. I cite the above not to convince you of my curious universal irresistability, but, rather, to suggest that my magnetism is not confined to the "visible. "

The park is most dark at that hour and yet I am never alone. Birds, cats, and certain rodents—albeit shy and well-mannered—are unable to keep away from me unless I constantly fire a small pistol I keep handy for just such occasions. Whenever I walk for exercise a dog will fall into step, running in and out of my direction, mile upon mile, until it drops dead from exhuastion. And, if another dog (or giraffe) tries to join me, it will instantly return to my side, growling the protective grudge of ownership. This is what bothers me most of all—the blind jealousy of those who would possess me. (I mentioned this to the girl—or, to one of several dozen beautiful and attractive girls at that time. I explained that she must

STORIES

learn to share like everyone else. Richard Burton had the same problem. Likewise, I am told, Spiro Agnew. I said, "Go get yourself Pat Boone or Raquel Welch for a change—I don't mind. " Yet, there is this ego thing which prevents our settling for second best. Ultimately, I was forced to beg her to stop coming around.)

With birds and fish—the lower animals, if you will—jealousy need not interfere with a brief, happy relationship. I may sit under a tree which, within moments, will be dangerously overloaded with sparrows, all wanting to hop inside my pockets where, you may be certain, I carry no crumbs or other bribes. But nevertheless, wherever I sit, panthers, jellyfish or snakes crawl lovingly over my entire person, and the birds are afraid to come down. Yet, they accept this. They wait their turn, grateful for even that privilege.

My reasons for telling you these things are, of course, complex and demanding; however, I think anyone is capable of comprehending some of my less cerebral observations. First of all, I wish it to be known that I am neither vain nor pompous; nor is this personal magnetism with which I am afflicted confined to the so-called "animated" things. For example, if I walk along the shore on a perfectly calm, sunny day, a breeze will spring up and follow me. Also (and this frequently happens) a fog will come in all the way from beyond the horizon and just hang around. Golf balls invariably roll toward me—this is one of my really major problems—golf balls. I never know from whence they come. They simply roll up and stop at my feet as though wishing nothing more in the world than to be petted. Yet, if I take the time to pet a golf ball it means that something else must be deprived—a watermelon, or perhaps a snail. Snails abound in the small garden nook where I usually sit reading dictionaires. They coat the pages with saliva, and one must take care not to close the book until the matter has had time to dry. Even so, I would just as leave pet a snail as a chrome fog-light. I practice impartiality at all times. There is the added problem of shrubs which also have this confounding desire for proximity and grow rapidly, entwining me even as I sit. I cannot trim them back. I do not believe in killing vegetables—they seem so naive, gentle and defenseless. I used to tell Miss Jaye about this, about my odd power over mind or matter. She was extremely jealous of snails—as women are so apt to be—and, in fact, of golf balls whenever I stooped to pick one up. I would say, "Say, Jaye—did I ever tell you my theory about it?"

"About what, " she would say—Jaye would say. "Say it again—that which you started to say. "

STORIES

And I would say to Jaye, "What did I start to say, Jaye?"

Say is a funny word if you say it too many times. I'd say this to her. I'd say, "say, Jaye—did you ever stop to think how funny it is to say "say" all day? The more you say "say, " the less it seems to say what it means— that is, say. "

Jaye, looking at me hungrily would say, "say—I thought you were going to tell me your theory — "

My theory is that all living things hover around human beings because we've got the Bomb and they haven't. But how to decide which things are living things? Certainly automobiles are more alive than musrooms or turtles—they go faster, make more sound, they shake and vibrate. Also, they die—autos. The thing is, they're trying to tell us something—the living things. That is why you got flies. They think we have the brains now (although we were all equal only a few billion years ago) and want us to stop wrecking the joint. That is especialy why things come up to me. They want me to do something about it . . .

When I tell this to psychiatrists they wait, unless there is a baseball game or war on.

I stand there trying to tell it while termites try to bore inside my shoes and the mice wait around hopefully. Soon, as always, a crowd forms. Naturally a police car stops nearby. It is a good time to mention the Bible now. I do. I say, "It's all in the Bible—go get Pat Boone to read it to you. " The cops leave you alone because they are afraid of Pat Boone and the Bible. I quickly walk away, followed by innumerable living things—small private planes, a lion or two, driverless cars, private detectives who can neither read nor write, and FBI men who incessantly click small, hidden cameras.

I had planned to mention that I was not going to mention cameras lest you get the impression that I am publicity-shy. Or, as Schopenhauer used to tell me, suffering from persecution. However, unauthorized people are constantly photographing me for the record.

As a rule they're these Golden Wedding couples who have motored all the way out to California to see it "live. " After Disneyland they cruise slowly up and down the Sunset Strip, collecting celebrities. If the temperature is between 72 and 84 they come to the coast at the rate of 1,398,729 per day. All of them are positive they have seen me on TV. I am, therefore, surrounded by grey, frizzled women who stand around in groups, having ancient orgasms while they click cheap Brownies at me.

STORIES

"Where have I seen you before?" they demand.
"Probably, " I answer mysteriously, giving them right profile.
"Aren't you on the Channel Seven?"
"I wouldn't know, " I reply, "I don't watch Channel Seven. "
In jail, where I go every two or three weeks, the first thing they do is take my picture, copies of which they bootleg around for ridiculous prices. At any jail I am always charged with leading a parade without a permit. I tell them that it wasn't a parade; it is no fault of mine that the masses insist upon being led. If there is a peace march or a civil rights demonstration, the cops come straight for me, demanding I stop it. I tell them I was simply on my way to the store to purchase several pounds of paperclips. Cynically, they'll want to know why I need so many paperclips, (the assumption being that I'm getting out some kind of heavy mailing for a subversive cause). When they ask, I take either the Fifth or First. Sometimes, for experimental purposes, I take the Seventh Amendment. It works better because the police don't know what the Seventh stands for (nor do I), but, on the other hand, they have heard about the First and Fifth which of course were written into the Constitution by hidden Communists. Usually on such occasions (my arrest) a handful of reporters will have fought their way through the mobs of well-wishers—their cameras wrecked, their faces bruised—and one is certain to ask me, "Do you believe in integration or disintegration?" It is one of those catch-questions like, Would You Want Your Sister To Marry Mahalia Jackson? Either way you answer, you're in trouble.

As to the pictures? They never appear in the papers. This is because of the following: 1) The reporters' cameras are damaged. 2) The reporters always come up afterwards and say, "Who are you?" "I'm someone else, " I tell them. They never believe it. They think I look like myself. But, as I explained, I merely happen to look like everyone else. Therefore, I never really know who I am until I have stopped being who I wasn't before I was . . .

Quite often, when pier fishing, I allot much of my attention to the problem of Me, which is the all of I that is really someone you've never met. (Certain doctors state that one has trouble relating to the whole if he just happens to be the sum of its parts.) However, even on lonely piers, in January, it is hard to concentrate; if there be but a dozen anglers, and the structure is 800 yards long, and I lower my fishline say, a hundred feet from the nearest angler, subtle changes occur. The wind starts up. Fog rolls in. Gulls and pelicans crowd me with their incessant screaming and pecking. Then, suddenly, at my right ear there will be a voice. It will say, "Oooooops! Pardon me!" From nowhere, you see, an angler has slunk. He is so close that his line has fouled mine. Probably, he will try to start a conversation about haircuts—planning, ultimately, to ask what I think about the Beatles, or Dr. Albert Schweitzer. He won't have the chance; already, another fisherman is talking loudly into my left ear. He wants to know what kind of bait I use. "Peanuts," I tell him.

"But do fish bite on peanuts?"

"I wouldn't know. I've never caught a fish."

It is true what I tell him. It is because I cannot bring myself to use hooks. This may seem curious to some until they understand that I cannot hurt slippery things. The fact I cannot is why so many will congregate around me, and is why the other angler suddenly pulls up a six-pound halibut, causing every fisherman on the pier to come on the run. Soon, I am being squeezed mercilessly. This is dangerous because I have claustrophobia whenever I am outdoors. That is my really only trouble—claustrophobia. It is the only reason I consent to therapy. (When I go without my consent it is merely because others have consented.) Naturally, psychologists are attracted to me like any of the others. They wish, mainly, to hear about my Research Program. Secretly, a lot of them think I am Herman Kahan or one of the great physicists, but traveling incognito. All of them are in need of help. I try to oblige. Gradually, they will edge around to suggesting, "Tell us about this gravitational power you exert over all things."

"It's nothing. Really, fellows —."

"But you are conducting scientific experiments —."

They have warmed their tape recorders, gotten out their pencils and pads. I caution them about overcrowding; they should fill as many of the back rows as possible so that others can get in. This accomplished, I go straight into my Popsicle Experiment. Popsicles are small, slippery, cold things people suck on. Much can be learned about a man (or woman) by keenly observing their relationship with the object in question. Of course, it is one thing to know why you do something. It is something else again if you can't stop. My research, however, deals with another aspect; that is, it is Sunday. I mean, say it's Sunday and I go up to a popsicle stand and the usual long line begins to form behind me but I don't ask for a popsicle. I am, obviously, expected to; crowds associate me with popsicles. However, I demand chop suey. A murmur escapes the crowd. Some, of course, will gig-

STORIES

gle. But it is a highpitched giggle—somewhere in the 14,000 cycle range, which means embarrassment. They don't know what to ask for now. Some just go up, cough, and ask for a loaf of bread. Others may want to know if they sell any golf balls there. A few will compromise and order Eskimo Pies, which incidentally, aren't even round. Still others will walk away frustrated—their afternoons ruined—and take out their hostilities on some unfortunate child-molester.

But it is when I hide behind the refreshment stand (disguised as a radio repair man) that the curious occurs; one by one people will go up and ask the attendant if he has any chop suey. "Hell no. " he will shout, "you think I'm crazy?" But after a while, he becomes less sure of himself. He begins to lace apology into his answer. Finally, (usually the 8th or 9th time) he is telling everyone that, starting next Monday, he is carrying a whole line of Oriental dishes.

The psychologists never tire of hearing me tell this.

Another of my contributions to science concerns tomato catsup which, on Thursdays, I pour onto a vanilla sundae. As in the previous project, the initial act is met with disillusion or revulsion, followed by ultimate acceptance, and, finally, the pleasure of sheer discovery. Even I—after witnessing the ecstatic expressions upon the faces of those trying the concoction—found it to be delicious.

This, of course, is what throws the analysts. Because they have already catalogued me as nonconforming—not one of the Group. Of course I'm not one of the Group; I *am* the Group. For this they have no historical answer. They merely glance at one another helplessly, and one of them is certain to inquire, petulantly, "Don't you feel just a little guilty—conducting these experiments? Playing around with human life?"

I of course have the normal guilts. But—since I am everyone—these must be called mass guilts. (This is not to be confused with the mass guilts suffered by Catholics who miss church; theirs is of a religious derivation which results in the hating of atheists, and atheists do not have to worry about masses. Yet, atheists and/or Unitarians also want me to share myself with them: often a Unitarian's front right tire will blow out just where I happen to be, which is in front of Erny's Drug Store. I never carry a spare; I don't want to have to lie when someone comes up and asks, "Got a 16.6x30 tubeless Nylon, Mister?" Should it be a girl Unitarian, she will be divorced, and insist she knows me from somewhere. "I've never been anywhere. " I answer resolutely, and start running.)

STORIES

About running. Running is my main problem other than walking. You can run only so long, then you have to stop. When you stop, some lonely person—usually a shoe clerk from Karl's—will set his bungalow afire. You've seen it happen a hundred times. He will affix you with an anxious, friendly glance. Then: "Excuse me, sir—have you seen a hook & ladder truck anywhere?" And now, because you're too exhausted to move, he'll suck you into intricate conversation about physical resemblances. Or even girls. It is a lonely indecent world. Because I happen to be most anybody, instead of myself, nobody will leave me alone until such time as I can learn to be someone who isn't anybody at all . . .

Just before I began to write this, a man threatened to leap from a skyscraper that happened to be across the street—obviously to ignite casual interest. Then, a beautiful girl in a trenchcoat came up (trenchcoats are another of my problems). She touched my sleeve and wistfully inquired to know if the man was my brother. I shook my head; I've no brothers—only imposters who would share my magnetism. "Then, " she pleaded, "could I see you alone for a minute—I mean, just you—yourself?" But you already know the answer to this; first, I am rarely myself. Secondly, the crowds had already formed, their pencils and autograph books held high over their heads, screaming and pressing. I don't know whatever became of the man who promised to jump. I was dangerous again, fighting to be myself, to save some little thing that was Me. Is it really so much to ask?

At this moment, it will do you absolutely no good to ask. The Exercise Yard is alive with guards carrying portable tape recorders, all of them masturbating furiously to capture my attention. This is what I actually, truthfully planned to discuss: tape recorders. Persons who play around with electronic gadgets invariably turn out to be, when examined, naked. You know as well as I that disrobers are, in reality, retrogressed voyeurs—even if of the opposite sex. Given the slightest opportunity they will approach complete strangers with loathsome schemes whereby his right to privacy will be ravaged. (Or is it "ravished?") I had hoped to discuss this also—but profound concentration becomes difficult when several whistles are being blown in unison. Furthermore, the members of the staff have begged me to deliver a talk to them at 4:38 p.m.—a most inopportune time since I shall be completely surrounded by volleyballs. Already several have bounced up and rolled to a stop. They rest there, waiting, smiling coyly. Powerless to leave unless I give them a rude, anguished shove, even as the attendants beckon to me with salacious gestures . . . their pencils held erect . . .

HOW TO BE PARALLEL

No.
No, I told them. Yes — I said no. But I know, now, that I was truer when I lied "yes" to my No. (Or was it No to *their* yes?) The answer is Never; I mean, the answer to their request as stated previously. No — under all circumstances could I say anything other than no. And yet, yes, it *is* a negative way of looking at everything — saying "no."

"Why," they wanted to know. Why 'no?' Why not 'Perhaps?' Perhaps *perhaps* (falling squarely between yes and no) was neither yes nor no, and yet manifests a more cooperative image . . . .

"Perhaps *perhaps* also could be construed as negative," Chairman Sniles had suggested.

A diminutive scientific man in a corduroy coat whose wide, flat face closely resembles frogs in their final stages? O, that is he. Cold chuckles came and went while he swung a vintage watch-fob counterclockwise. "If —" he continued, "if you suffered from dandruff, and asked your doctor if there was a chance of recovering, and he said 'perhaps,' you would consider it quite, quite negative."

Whereupon the chairman bent, retied, then untied his right and left shoes. They were, I noticed, a matched pair; but frankly black, very off-season. Even blue was secondary to orange. The thought came to me that the man might be falling behind in his payments. If he were, then I should be confounded by sympathy, delighted to cooperate. During this thought Niles straightened, bumping his head against a table (which I took to be one of those amazingly realistic mahogany plastics). Now his hair contracted with pain, but he said, "You get the symbolism?"

No, I told him, no. Symbolism escapes me.

"Did you say no? Yes?"

"Yes." I glanced oblongly at the shoes of the other committeemen. Predictably, they were into greens and yellows. "Yes" — I said, "I don't get the symbolism." Representative Turncloude spoke. He drives a Bentley carefully disguised as a Chrysler. He is not afraid to be found anywhere,

STORIES

at all times, and operates a duck-hunting club in Louisiana when not serving his country. Turncloude, himself, always voted "yes" on everything. A positive thinker — already famed for his scholarly essay on cement — he had personally offered to send a free American flag to every needy family in his constituency if they couldn't afford one. As a former Judge he'd been known as a man of deep and lengthy convictions. Now, as he spoke, I recalled that while campaigning he had come out strongly in favor of water. At the same time he was against hit & run driving, vowed to outlaw suicide, and was opposed to child-molestation in any form. He was "negative" about heroin, sociology, and faulty wiring. He was a staunch opponent of ill health; he campaigned tirelessly against crooked repair men and budgets. "Budgets," he once confided to a convention of laundrymen (who would later leak it to the National Inquirer) "are ivory tower schemes put together by men who've no money in the bank and would like to put the rest of us in the same fix."

8:05 Monday

Chairman Sniles! Remember him as key speaker at the Fellowship Of Overhead Garage Door Hangers in Atlantic City? Perennially inspirational, militantly optimistic, he shared this wisdom with his audience:

"Just what's the difference between an optimist and a pessimist? The optimist is a guy that sees all women lying in bed naked. A pessimist is a jerk that don't think he ever will!" The standing ovation is said to have been clocked at 17 minutes and 49 seconds, Daylight Saving Time. Turncloude himself (at that time head of a small chimney-sweeping firm) personally congratulated the speaker, adding a few carefully chosen words about unswerving loyalty to the challenge. It takes discipline and patience to install overhead doors. As he said, " . . . when you face the harsh reality of coiled spring-steel you're all alone out there on the firing lines. You got to believe in liberty & equality. There are no atheists in garage door situations . . . . . "

(Here it becomes obvious that the Senator got his metaphors scrambled. He was discussing two unrelated topics, unaware that neither had anything to do with naked women. May I beg to explain this? Although a man of terrifying energy, Turncloude long ago trained himself to doze throughout other men's speeches in order to conserve strength for the greater, more pressing problems confronting the American way.) Again, sleep probably prevented him from hearing facts or statistics which might contaminate the purity of a man's own conclusions. It is a good policy to keep one's self innocent of too much knowledge —

12:34 PM Thursday

I was quite aware that once the committee members had reassured one another of their dedication and loyalty, they'd again focus their attention upon me; they would want to know if I understood the delicate symbolism implied in Sniles' disarmingly simple axiom. I had decided to say "perhaps," feeling that by answering "no" I would risk falling into the trap of intellectual partisanship.

If I said "perhaps" or "perhaps so" they would all feel better, and someone would suggest it was a good time for a break — coffee, or perhaps alfalfa sprouts. They would have to remove my strait-jacket then because I resist being force-fed. They are aware of this; you see, Dr. Smoor is the type of therapist who will stop suddenly in a corridor, pretend to dust his shoes with a soiled handkerchief, then stand upright and whisper confidential information to whoever happens to be nearby. Oddly, Smoor's shoes become dustier when the listener happens to be a committeeman. He will say, "Number 3997-D had a wet dream last night." Or, "Number 3998-E must be allowed free use of his genitals during lunch." Sometimes, Dr. Smoor drops paper messages containing a pleasant adverb or two. One that I confiscated read: "Miss Dlfgrrlwp! May I come watch your bowel movement some time?" Ordinarily he is a specialist in female defecation, yes, but of late he has taken a special interest in me — that's my trouble — defecation.

It started when I went on a hunger strike for thirty days in the old Atlanta cell block. The bone-aches began then, and, I suppose, the hallucinations. I kept dreaming I was out. Then, later, when I *was* out, I kept dreaming I was *in*. This is the worst thing about being free after long periods of incarceration — you're never sure it's not a trick of the mind. You might be riding along in a Jaguar convertible and, of a sudden, wake up to find yourself lying on a cot in cell nine. You are never to know for sure because there is absolutely no way to prove that freedom isn't a wonderful dream. For the rest of your life you are to go on, wondering: Am I outside? Or in?

"Well? Does the suspect care to answer or not?"

Even now I had been dreaming, for I had not heard the question. I had been dreaming that I was *dreaming* I was a prisoner, and that, in reality, I was "out" — sailing a small boat. I asked them to repeat the question.

"There's only a hair of difference between 'perhaps' and 'maybe.'" Professor Sniles brought from his corduroy coat pocket an orange yo-yo. He dangled it enticingly before me. "Think you could go for 'maybe' instead of 'perhaps?'"

I said "maybe."

"Maybe what?"

"Maybe *perhaps*."

Sniles had been a minor Bass fisherman before joining the staff. Now he smiled and it was again noticeable that his lips went on endlessly — far to the right, even farther to the left. One could have inserted a butterplate into his grin. I am not certain; I've not seen a butterplate in two years. We use cardboard oleomargerine plates here.

"Look before you leap!" McBaine admonished, "He who hesitates is lost!" Did I explain McBaine? He mounts small animals in a taxidermist's shoppe when not dissecting lunatics for the probation department. Predictably, he would intimidate me later; but sooner than that he went over to the wall and stroked a busily moulting bald eagle which forever was destined to clutch a handful of five dollar bills in its talons. The plaque underneath muttered something about honoring James Audubon, father of our country. An alert Boy Scout warned him that George Washington was our first President. He giggled amiably, then slid one of the bird's glass eyes into his breast pocket. Two feathers started to float to the carpet — (a prematurely lavender purple) — then caught a thermal and made it to the ceiling.

"If everybody plucked just one feather from a consenting eagle every time there was an investigation — and investigations continue at the present rate — they'd have to get another one in nineteen months. Or, exactly one year and seven weeks from the time I threw a guard at the television set in Lewisburgh." (Quotes mine.)

I'll not belabor the charge that I've a fascinating mind. However, the fact that a man collects or puts together important information like the above should not be lauded as a "personal" achievement. Even Sir Edward Einstein (or do we mean Alfred?) attributes brilliance to so little a factor as "hard work" and long hours at the multiplication table.

3:45 Friday

The clock in the board room is synchronized with Pentagon time. I picketed in front of the Democratic stronghold in 1983, although I forget why. Was it because of the Boer War? Or because privates in the trenches were not served hot lunches during the heraldic battle of Bull Run?

3:46

It is true I've kept dossiers on all the committee members. I shall use this information in the event that they do not care to turn themselves in. Turncloude, McBaine and Sniles have been mentioned. There remain others: Warner — a Trapezoidal, zebra-faced man — has a convoluted kneecap and plays around with Twinkies. Col. Wolfffgang Heseman Utt is said to snare young girls from their idling Buicks, drag them into bushes and snogger them several times each. The secretary, Miss Dlbyknr, speaks phonetically, comes to work wearing nasty underthings, and is left-handed at all times. Mike Chord was once active in the Existentualist movement; however the charges were dropped and he presently serves as Junior Persecutor. Warden J.J.J.J. Braker, of course, has full veto power. He has been with the prison system for several decades; ten years as an inmate, then fourteen as administrator. His wife was found dead in the boudior of an Arabian tentmaker back in the '60's. Arabella Diston (of Wright & Diston) sits in on special occasions such as mine. She is a chronic New Yorker, loaths sycamore trees, and jogs openly.

These, then, are those who sit in judgement of my present and future. Will I be charged with snoggery, then released for excellent behavior? Will Chord inform everyone that I was caught driving an imported car at the time Chrysler was going bankrupt? And the submarine charge — it was eventually dismissed, yes, but once a man has jeopardized national security he's never forgiven. The fact that I had two Japanese stereo sets (one for Tuesdays and Wednesdays and the other for holidays) will be brought up. McBaine will nibble away on this, even mentioning that I was wearing Italian shoes and had a Hong Kong tailor when they fingerprinted me. Commissioner Warner may "p-s-s-s-s-t" to the clerk that I threatened to turn off my electricity if they built the Nuclear power plant at John Wayne Inlet; the clerk would then declare a recess, after which someone would ask if all my kitchen appliances were made in America. (I'd take the Sixth Amendment since the Fifth is a frank confession of guilt.)

4:56 Monday

No. They're unable to come to a decision.

STORIES

2:54 Tuesday

Perhaps! Perhaps the new deputy will bring chaos out of order — he replaces Col. Utt who was fouled while playing soccer. I no longer know about No because new committeemen replace the old, wornout members. A murmer of applause escapes the lips of Warden Beaker who claps with his mouth instead of hands. He expects to replace Turncloude in the Spanking Department should the dedicated patriot die in office as a martyr to freedom. No, I'm unable to tell you which crime I'm being tried for; either the law is forever against me, or everything I do is forever against the law. However, I have never kissed a guard. I am not now — nor have I ever been — the owner of a car made in Central America. I was paroled to prison ten years ago, but put on probation there. Because of crowded conditions I was forced to share solitary confinement with 22 other prisoners, all of them talking in phoney Greek accents, none of them very affectionate. One had been a Footlocker for the Cascadians in the Peacemaker Campaign. Another wets his pants each time he mentions sniggling Apes in Kimbrona valley. One man boasts of rowing his samovar across Sultanic Bay while still a young girl, where he leeched a Ferro. All of them want to have moonlight fall upon their naked thighs, believing that Ulysses will lead them to a nunnery — where no down payment is required. Their symbolism was reasonably symbolic; yet, moonrays leak through our bars only once in a blue moon or, specifically, Thursdays at 11:03 P.M.

11:03 Thursday P.M.

We're running late sitting here while the chairperson does kneejerks to the rhythm of *'Do It Again, Sam'* (very popular in the free world for an entire night in 1984). The bald eagle, now "Naked as a Jaybird," as officer Follopp puts it, has a new, recycled eye! Actually, it is a quartz chip lovingly donated by the poor children of Ethiopia as a gesture of appreciation for the right to watch American gangster movies on pirated video. It winks solemnly every time someone here tells a fib. I've personally figured it should last many years because so far it has never opened.

11:20 Thursday P.M.

Just now! Yes! O, indeed yes — the eagle's final, conclusive feather floated carpet-ward like the last leaf of autumn! And McBaine, with a model Mark VII ashtray, caught it. However, during an undesired moment,

STORIES

Congressman Oddbold sneezed; the feather became airborne, then gently came to rest on the left shoulder of Commissioner Drodge. This I statistically computed to be one of those mathematical miracles, for Drodge absolutely has no shoulders. He is a huge, tapering man; a chianti bottle — often mistaken for De Gaulle by small nearsighted boys. No one seemed able to tell Drodge of his predicament. He's an important man — keen about sewers and other public works. He owned Puente, California, and a matching set of bannisters. He was honorary chairman of the League To Prevent Blackbirds. Also he legislated for years (albeit unsuccessfully) against octopus, believing them a pest and nuisance. He was not a man to whom one could easily say, "There is an eagle feather on your shoulder — no, the other shoulder." This caused the committee members to glance about nervously; McBaine got out a filter cigarette and lit the middle. Turncloude pushed himself back from the long table, looked down, and said to Professor Sniles, with irritation in his voice, "You're wearing black shoes." Sniles warned Oddbold (who had sneezed and started the whole thing) "Better do something for that cold! Colds can be dangerous —" Oddbold, I felt deeply sorry for; he impetuously grasped Professor Sniles' orange Yo-Yo, put it inside his mouth and closed his lips. About ten inches of string hung out. I was afraid that, were he to sneeze again, the thing would be projected with lethal velocity. And Turncloude was sitting directly in harm's way. I knew what my group therapist would say about this: "There *are* no accidents! Why would a man given to sneezing just happen to place himself across from someone he loathed and place a Yo-Yo in his mouth?"

Turncloude, it's suspected, had been warned of psychology and its fringe para-gyricalations, or, perhaps, he may have been keenly sensitive to the vicissitudes of others. At any rate he said, "Maybe we should *all* go out and put a little something in our mouths — might clear the air a bit."

Sniles said, "You mean like lunch, Senator?" The others took turns repeating variations on his declamation (except Oddbold who remained stoic but uneasy). I noticed that all but six inches of string had disappeared. I prophesied that they would ask me if *I* would like lunch. Another catch question; I'd had nothing to eat but Oklahoma laminated duck L'Orange with a light Mexican sherbert for several weeks; they'd trick me into uttering the word "yes." They asked : Turncloude said, "Think a Caeser Salad would look good on you, sir?"

"I'm a vegetarian," I replied successfully.

Sniles said, "They put out a pretty goldarned good old meatless Veal

143

Escallopini at the 265 Club, boy — "
"No," I told them, "no."
"*Baseball,* man!" Oddbold unexpectedly removed the Yo-Yo from his mouth and wound up for the pitch. Regrettably, he'd forgot to take the end of the string out; it twirled hurriedly back and disappeared inside his mouth with a *phulf.* Sniles said, "Like, see — we would catch the last two innings at the TV bar."
Yes, I told them "no" again.
"Bet it's like years since you tore into Pizza-pie with Long Island dressing, eh? — We'd take off your handcuffs maybe if you're a good boy —"
I said "One year and 14 months. I had a vintage Pierce Arrow with wire wheels all around."
"Hah! But you never rode in a stretched chauffeur-driven Abraham Lincoln Continental!" McBaine had cut clear across me now. He exchanged eyes with Oddbold for an uncertain length of time. Then, unsatisfied with the trade, he placed them on Turncloude who didn't seem to notice; for he added, "Bet they didn't let you eat with a real knife made out of real metal—"
"No," I told them. No, the answer has to be no.
"But I remember a tossed salad in Illinois. I was picketing the income tax building and went into this little restaurant. It was really tossed —"
"Think of that!" Turncloude exclaimed, searching the others to make certain they were paying attention. At that moment I could think of nothing to say so I said, "Representative Drodge — there's an eagle feather on your shoulder."
"What?"
"Eagle feather."
"Oh." He looked warily at Turncloude. "Where?"
"On your shoulder. No — other shoulder."
He looked, but of course he couldn't see either shoulder because there aren't any. It was then that Sniles got up, handsomely picked it off, and was about to place it on the blank sheet of paper beside the sharp pencil, when Oddbold sneezed again. Once more the feather was air-borne. Turncloude had, impossibly, fallen asleep again to conserve his energy for preventing the free world from becoming enslaved. The sneeze awakened him. He yawned — the feather was sucked in. His mouth — as I have mentioned — is wide-spread; he was unaware that the feather dwelt inside it now. The rest of us were sharing a common shame — another's tragedy

which must be borne in secret. McBaine looked over at me sadly and winked. Drodge — embarrassed but loyal to the end — pointed to the wall and said, "That's some eagle!" Oddbold remarked, "Some people are allergic to eagles! I had an aunt in Montana who used to sneeze every time one flew over the farm." Sniles said sneezing was common in his family which, incidentally, came here on the U.S.S. Mayflower and were related to Miles Standish although having been many times removed. This remark set me to thinking about foreigners; if foreigners aren't patriotic zealots, they're probably not Armenians. I can usually identify immigrant families by the number of American flags they display: If they have three or more they've only recently arrived and can't speak English. (McBaine is an exception; his home displays Old Glory every day of the year — but always at half mast; this is because Americans are constantly dying away and every loss of a taxpayer indirectly aids the enemy.)

11:59

Regarding Snile's family — if they really came over on the H.M.S. Mayflower, and they're really so loyal, why are they always being removed? I decided to dwell upon this shortly after nightfall but before they turn off the Pepsi-Cola machine. At midnight, everybody goes to the lavatory where the fun starts.

2:42 A.M.

Do you realize that I have been digressing in my favor?

Extended periods of incarceration develop in the prisoner an ability to imagine total reality; once, when #91675 stabbed a guard, I levitated throughout the entire performance by insisting I was away, fishing on the mudflats of Oyster Bay. No one was around. A clear, cold, sad beautiful afternoon with a few migrating ostriches. And an ice-cream vendor who'd driven there for no apparent reason and run over a lobster. The guard, allegedly, had fallen at my feet. Mike had shouted, "My God — the sonofabitch tripped and hurt himself!" Afterwards, I was privileged to talk like an eyewitness. But I told them *No.* "No," I told them, "I didn't see a thing except a pair of lesbian mermaids. No — put me in solitary! Take away my Twinkie privileges! Do as you wish! My answer is no. And no lo contendre, either!"

Nowadays No is usually more right than wrong; every week there are more and more things we should be saying "no" to but instead we say "yes,"

STORIES

or "oh, heck." We shrug. Everybody else is saying Yes. But where, I ask, are we all going? To lunch at the 365 Club?

3:55 P.M.

This is what the stenographer didn't want to know. She was raised in the prosperous village of Mondale-On-The-Hudson where her father sold tickets for the local Capitalist Day Parade. Dr. Smoor had sent her in. If we were to have luncheon at the Club there were certain intimate details; if they removed the prisoner's straight-jacket, he was wearing pajamas. If they took off the pajamas, well — you know. And the people at the 365 behave indecently toward customers who come for the $89.89 Special still wearing jumpsuits or knickerbockers; it's one of those conservative Hawaiian Hardtops with Rain Forests and waterfalls and Oriental high-jumpers racing around in bamboo bikinis. I was there for several moments in 1978 when I tried, unsuccessfully, to take a Filipino.

Smoor's stenographer now hovered delicately over the Senator whose elbows hinted of sex: "Shall I dress the prisoner out —" She paused. "— Or?"

Turncloude started to answer, but just then the feather shot out of his mouth. Wet, it fell to the table where all of us watched ashamedly. Oddbold was first to act. With an angry thrust, he grabbed, then stuffed the mortifying thing into his coat pocket. Now he stared at me with genuine fear; he was afraid I was going to say, "Senator Turncloude! A feather just flew out of your mouth! Mr. Oddbold has it in his coat pocket!" (I, too, was afraid I would say it.) And like some premonitions, the fear was justified. Distinctly I heard my own voice (although as if pretending it were mine) cough, then announce clearly, "Senator Turncloude! A feather just flew out of your mouth!" I did, however, refrain from telling him who had it. I am not now, nor have I ever been, a stoolpigeon concerning feathers. That is why they keep me on here. Turncloude stared at me, absolutely baffled. I read sheer terror on the faces of everyone present, and I distinctly smelled McBaine who was three feet to my windward. Yet, no one was able to say anything. We waited; my communication passed inwardly past the Senator's ears, met rejection and disbelief, but loitered there, arguing plaintively. Oddbold was first to speak. He thrust the Yo-Yo at me and almost shouted, "Here! You want this Yo-Yo?"

No, I told him, no. Thank you, no.

"Why not? They make good pests."

(I am not certain he said this last. But he *looked* like the kind of man capable of saying such a thing. More probably, the phrase is recalled from far back in my childhood — perhaps farther back than Dr. Smoor ever hopes to go with me. Once someone had offered me an octopus down at the tidepools; they kept trying to place it in my pockets although I was naked.)

(Since I have disgressed again, kindly indulge a few more items on Turncloude which have just come in. I mean, something triggered them. Going to the bathroom triggers certain things in likewise people. When they used to let us shave, with razors, whenever I stood before the mirror, I had a golden scene of myself walking from the car near Campo, California. It was where pines take over from the oaks, I had my bass rod in hand, and the dust was light, hot, dry, and there was this mountain aroma. There was a girl also, but she was far away in another dream — moist dream. Actually, I was alone, but I had this dream that, somehow she was with me. We would walk toward this pond that was never there just when you needed it. I forget what happened because some malcontent ate the mirror.)

No. You are right! No — it is true! Yes — I have already digressed from my digression! I was starting to tell more about the committee head, Turncloude, when, no! — my mind cast loose its moorings and began this long, aimless drift. I know that I cannot say "no" to this — the charge that I have evaded! Evaded! No. Absolutely yes!

I shall, then, tell. Turncloude is a master baiter. He is afraid of chicken sandwiches on Wednesdays. He discriminates against Turkish flying machines. *Constantly!* Leaky faucets — if within one hundred feet of hearing — give him hydrophobia. He has for years tried to bring buttonhooks back into vogue. His duck club, which he runs for profit, has a high rate of shooting accidents. Yet, Turncloude has been chief investigator for thirty-two years. He was big on the air in the late sixties when he conducted the sensational Kleenex Investigations. I remember him. I wasn't there. But I saw that face on a 13-inch screen, with its wider smile. Often the smile came right into your living room. His yawn caused viewers to get larger TV sets so they could see the rest of him. The rest was less copacetic: When angered at a suspect, Turncloude's eyebrows suddenly welded, then shot skyward where, for a full minute of valuable sponsored time, they achieved omniscience. Then his voice crashed through, destroying everything within range. On a normal night he could break five witnesses before it was time for the first commercial. Small, odd, innocuous details became

STORIES

towering incriminations before the cold leer, the aghast eye. A man might blurt out that he had been eating popcorn at a Japanese movie on the evening in question. This called forth a tidal wave of associations from the Investigator's brooding mind. Often, Turncloude wept unabashedly while a suspect confessed he had been hoodwinked into attending an NAACP meeting; a virtual electrical storm followed, punctuated by thunder, and the fatal lightning of the Senator's tongue. Even the audience became morbidly involved; a man in Iowa, driving his car and tuned to the broadcast, suddenly (according to the AP) pulled over to the curb, scrawled a suicide note, and drove over an embankment. A Michigan plumber watching the program (on channel Nine) got up, walked quietly down to the police precinct and turned himself in. "I just began to feel filthy," he told the booking clerk, "I need to be locked up for a while." On the night Turncloude broke the Board Of Education the FBI was besieged with telephone calls by persons who insisted on confessing to crimes they had not committed Several children, including a Palestinian Liberal, turned their parents in. Housewives in Atlanta got together and removed all the canned Chow Mein from a local super market. A Unitarian minister in New Jersey cancelled his prepared sermon on Share-croppers and, instead, conducted prayers for the MX Missile. "Everybody is guilty of *some*thing," a college philosopher summed up. "Reminds you of Mark Twain's famous practical joke. It's good we have a man like Turncloude around — sort of clears the air of misguided dialectic pollution." Shortly afterward he was made Chancellor of an elitist southern military Academy where he personally conducted bayonet practice.

There're subtler side effects of the Senator's impassioned oratory; some 2,885 Senior Citizens marched (or were carried) to some 46 recruiting centers where they offered to enlist. A Black insurance broker turned in his Rolls Royce and ordered three Fords. An Iranian rug importer — catching only the end of a recycled broadcast — tried to have himself deported to West Germany. He was only relatively successful because thousands there (listening to Turncloude's *Free America* program) reluctantly came to the conclusion that they were Socialist sympathers and belonged in Cuba. The rug merchant now peddles stuffed eagles on street corners somewhere in Wales according to my sister-in-law.

3:57 A.M. Sunday

An alternative to "Yes," "No" or "Perhaps" is for the defendant to say,

"I don't remember," or "I'm simply furious with myself but I'll be jiggered if I can't recall who I was with where on the star-studded evening you mention." If they can't bring in someone from the Mental Telepathy Squad — or a low-cost hypnotist — you're home free. Or at least on probation. With your generous permission I illustrate:

You stand accused of smiling during a vigil in front of the U.N. Building. (Or committing Macrame in a crowded theater. Or personally irrigating some withered old hibiscus in a vacant lot — it doesn't matter.) Regardless what preliminary questions are levelled they'll ask "What did you do on Martin Lutheran King Day?" If you say "I prayed." Or, "I bought a banjo from a poor old shoe-shine boy whose cousin is a Numbers Runner," your file will be turned over to the Texas Rangers. But if you can't remember Dr. King's birthday at all you are just an ordinary American — not unlike those who forget anniversaries, alimony payments, speed limits, bridge scores or capital gains.

You can get a year and a day for committing murder or stepping in front of a trolley car carrying nuclear ammunition. I did. Maybe I didn't. But I did get 366 days. I'm not certain why they keep me around in here — some say I wickedly murdered an ancient lady beekeeper; others claim I was a practicing boat robber. Some rumors have me forging draft cards, or smuggling sugar to diabetes patients, or, even, leading an expeditionary force into the Pentagon.

And, once out, you're still in. Wherever you go they're waiting for you to trip. You can trip over a suspended driver's license, a bottle of Seagram's Crown on a beach, a room with a girl, a girl with a record. Dr. Smoor is trying to prove that I am guilty of all the preceding charges, and guilty by insanity. All I must do when he probes is say "perhaps." Did I really hate the C.I.A. or was it Mother all along? What was my *real* motivation for lying down in front of the Capitalist Day Parade? Because they disapprove of people who squander their money on Russian Plays? Or because I was sleepy? Do I loathe McBaine because he refuses to embrace ball players of inferior color unless they lose? Or is it simply because I hated Father instead of Mother when he slept with my sister? Should I glance convincingly at Dr. Smoor and say, "I don't remember, perhaps?"

6:23 Wednesday

One day, while in solitary confinement, he visited me. A highly important man, Smoor is allowed to wear Alaskan sports shirts and two-tone shoes. He would come into my cell, perspiring, and say, "Whew! Hot enough for you?" Everything becomes cheery, confident and businesslike when he is nearby. He exhudes optimism about the inside because mostly he is outside. Yet I, who am an outsider, am kept inside. "The whole thing is to learn how to be parallel," he announces confidently, "That's democracy! We don't have to be exactly like the other fellow but all must move in the same direction together —"

I remind him, "That's what the Romans said. They were very parallel."

"You didn't have to commit civil disobedience! Nobody made you tresspass onto the missile base! There are other ways to be effective —"

"Perhaps." Perhaps maybe there are.

But as Dr. Smoor crouches in my humid cell, sweating out his accrued rationalizations, he becomes Senator Turncloude. He becomes McBaine, Drodge, Oddbold, Sniles. I am no longer certain any of them ever existed. Probably all of them are my invention — a revenge fantasy played out during linoleum commercials. (You cannot play "Solitary" in solitary confinement. It is too dark. There are no cards.) Yes! All of them are the common enemy — unseen and imagined — like Fascists, businessmen, Negroes, Communists, Jews, Cadillacs, Catholics, child-molesters, addicts, squares, vegetarians. A man must have something to hate in order to keep from hating himself. Mike Johnson, before his execution, played it the other way; he laughed. And the doctors laugh when they read my FBI transcript; it is so filled with titillating adventures. Often, one of them will stop before my cot and ask me. He will ask, if maybe, perhaps, I'm not just a shade or two left of right. This is my big scene.

"No!" I tell him, "No! Not at all! No — my answer to that is no! No! A thousand times no!" Yes! My answer is *No.* I *know* it's no! No maybe or perhaps about it —

But when the iron door clangs shut there are still eighteen months, three weeks and 21 hours. The doctor has only shortened your sentence a few moments. You do hard-time now because some link with the outside world was temporarily re-established. You must become used to the blackness again, and the sound of your own heart in this deathly silence. Worst of all is the renewed, violent struggle with your own thought process — the whirled torture of anguish. But if you can re-invent Senator Turncloude with an eagle feather in his mouth you can make yourself laugh. Perhaps . . . . .

STORIES

8:49 P.M. Sunday

A long standing prison rule has been suspended! We are now allowed to read the telephone directories! Yes — even the Yellow Pages. Once again the pulse — the very heartbeat — of this grand country of ours is at my fingertips. From A to Z I'm again able to identify with the taxpayer who needs carpet-cleaners, tropical fish, chrome-plating, pianos, tree surgery, psychiatric counselling, lamp shades, rewiring, takeout Burritos, roofing, high-powered rifles, skates, art instruction, religion, cement, yachts, foam rubber, snowploughs . . . .

You're aware that reading privileges can be suspended if the inmate falls below 79 points on the Capone Model Prisoner Chart? Yes! But a recent Supreme Court decision ruled that all felons shall be allowed to retain their God-given normal characteristics — hate, anger, revenge, hunger, thirst, day (and wet) dreams, and memory. This is why I've set about to memorize every word and number in the Yellow Pages. I've already got to the top of page 93 which begins with Aardvark: "By simply dialing 442-6007 you can have your aardvark repaired by conscientious, honest experts at an astonishingly low cost."

Obviously I'll need Yachts when I get out. Yes, and Tropical Fish, Cement, Chrome-Plating, French Lessons. Probably I'll need Re-Wiring and Tree Surgery. Why not an Aardvark? Dr. Woolfffgang Utt says in his book *(A Layman's Guide to Confabulating Neo-Elipses in Dextroamphetic Coaxuals Among Reciprocatingualistic Parolees)* " . . . . once the criminal is forced back into normal society he'll start buying things and having them repaired . . . "

Yes. Perhaps No should be Yes perhaps.

POETRY

STANDING AGHAST IN THE TENSE PRESENT IMPERFECT

Other than that
There were no sand bars during the afternoon
A cathedral had found its way down to the waterfront;
Lingered there, awaiting pigeons or bats
And a flock of hang-gliders settled among the Plaza trees
With no reasonable hope for updrafts.
Along the embarkadero a fobbed old man
Pushed his life ahead in a shopping cart
  I had noticed a snail in the gardens of Dr. Knoble
  It had upped periscopes and was mowing his ivy
  The Doctor was out: golf.
  I was aware that the townspeople still went
    around
  Trying to make themselves thin: that they
  Continued to erase history whenever possible
  So that the neoprene sidewalks
    Could carry the Majority.
  But few of the many who sell rowboats were
    available
More of them had less to say about the economy
Though a girl with the body of a heron
Who sat an inflatable life-raft — sat it helpfully —
Spoke of the growing market in combustibles.
Other than that,
There were unclassified things that sucked or snorted
Among the marsh's elders;
Not mergansors discovering the new sexuality;
Nor tennis jocks seeking lost balls.
Think, instead, of condos sprung against the sky;
Know a pelican for each whitewashed statue
And enough barracuda to go around, or,
Of bottomless girls riding gay dolphins
  Through giggling breakers.
 — And what of noble swains
  Tearing up the mudflats in blown Chevvies
  Fishing for shreiks and

POETRY

>   *Forcing cottontails to make jackrabbit starts?*
You knew it all;
But let's hear it for
Oilbound ducks in flightless awe
>   *Back-pedaling the tide.*
While
Purple bivalves spurt love at one another
Beyond reach of eight licensed clam-diggers;
Knew tradesmen, knew electric, mouth, and hand organs
But merely surmised the unmentionable.
Note that instant Veal Scaloppine remained available,
That endangered species still shopped for corkscrews.
That uninhabited soft-drink cans rested lightly
>   *Upon snargled scrub*
As if expecting helium, and with it,
Ingenius little voyages to the moon.
There were fewer now than in the pleasant times;
Not many discarded mattresses; a real shortage
>   *Of haikus and asparagus*
And yet men still went up to each other
And fumbled around in restricted zones,
And young ladies with signature asses
Talked of office mischief,
>   *Or cholesterol,*
Even as airliners dunked and skidded in reasonable ways
>   *I? I continued standing aghast;*
>   *Staunch defender of nothing at all*
>   *Withholding a vote*
>   *For the invisible future*
>   *For the past-imperfect*
>   *The tense present.*
The high school's to be removed
To make room for a Jacuzzi; we're going ahead.
There's to be less waste in the libraries,
Fewer leftovers on Senior Citizens' plates
Fewer legs crossed for Junior executives.
We're going ahead.
A waitress with a neutered alligator's physique

And a salesman of guaranteed vasectomies
Order diamonds from page 18,203 of the Sears catalogue
Aware that everything, homicide excepted,
Takes a little longer tonight,
Lasts shorter, costs higher,
And is narrowly received with widening eye.
    We're going ahead.
A grandfather of five, in shorts,
Jogs his memory down shady lanes
Curtailed by sniffing dogs
And dreaming up Stanley Steamers.
    Before resigning entirely
    I talked over my problem with the row-boat people.
    They described reassuring new weaponry
    That will take the place of fine restaurants
    And medical attention.
    A few thought inflation would be wiped out,
    And prosperity, and housing, and the enemies
        Of Freedom;
    And, even ourselves.
    Other than that there's nothing to worry ab . . .

POETRY

REFUGIO PASS

Fish swam & sank where an ocean
Ran away from its islands and
Two minutes later
The Indians
Came & went
And the flora oriented itself
Learned to love drought, clay, desert air and
To build with cloudbursts in mind.
All animals squeaked, pounced, squatted
And became what they became
In an hour's paleontology
And an entire day passed after that
For time slept until men with their machines
Their worrying, hurrying sets of wheels
Commenced to write small scars
Upon the part
Of the whole that meant everything
To everything, promising that fifteen minutes hence
A coyote's contour would be altered
And oriented until it became
What it must become.

ON A GIVEN THURSDAY OF THE YEAR

Note:
Mockingbirds with their strict, measuring glance
And snails ejected by the tide itself; then insects
Under glass,
Buzzing tirelessly.
Then the lost looks of love on all dogs
    Coiled unsprung on their porches
        To dream of unarmed magazine salesmen.
And a season of abandoned cats which came heavy
    With the burden of
    No.
Later, it was civilization cooking breakfast
For a pair of tired Cops.
And a disabled survivor of some
    War,
    Traffic accident,
    Disease or fire
Overcompensating from door to door
While cautious men along the thorofare go 'round
Making big thoughts into little ones.
    There were turtles which had blundered
        into gutters;
    Women whose tires failed,
    Pilots whose chutes didn't open,
    Yachts with no wind, and
    Children raised under the wink of
        progressive education;
Always the go-between for yourself
And the life advertised.
    -And watermelons pried open with crowbars
    And toastmasters left in the fields to rot
    And they held up a mirror
    And the reflection was
You. You? You . . .

POETRY

SATURDAY AFTERNOON, FIVE O'CLOCK

They're doing something pretty exciting over there
Down at Val-Con, fellows,
Making a thing
To go onto the thing
That'll put the Guess-What
Clear into the You-know-where.

And I think they've got the drop on the Reds, Whites, Blues
      And Yellows, fellows
          This time.
And between you
And me
      It's quite a drop.
But of course —
It's supposed to be hush-hush and all that —
But of course —
      Between you and me
      They aren't fooling anybody when they pretend
      To be making
Balance wheels for women's watches, or outboard motors.
Therefore,
I don't think I'm giving anything away
      or anything
When I mention it in passing here that actually, factually
They're up to their ears and nose-cones on this X
That fits on the Y
That triggers the thing
On the guess-what hush-hush.

Therefore,
If somebody'll make me another
      Only more ice and less soda this time
I'll really break down and tell you a couple of things
About the thing
They're doing down at Val-Con, fellows.

A PREFACE TO THE INTRODUCTION TO A PHILOSOPHICAL TREATISE ON COMPARATIVE ECONOMICS

"What do they do when they do that which they do
When they're doing it
   Down
At Amalgamated Fabrications, Inc."
The East Indian student
From Carnegie Tech
  Asked, and was answered,
   'Plan the new! All new! So very, very new
    Oldsmobile hubcap.'
This they said,
Oh, certainly said —
As though unable to detect some hairline difference
Between bragging and confessing.

  It was a fine, bold, obsolescent afternoon
  For the orientation of Occidentals
  And the student turned off his Japanese tape recorder
  And ignited a Mexican cigarette
  With his German lighter and said Oh.
 He was thinking East; southeast by a quarter east.
 He was thinking all right, thinking,
How many meals could be cooked along the Ganges River
In last season's outdated hubcaps—
  Were there something to cook; or,
How much rain could be gathered
If all the hubcaps of all Oldsmobiles were laid end to end
Across the Punjab?
  "About a million litres!" He exclaimed wonderously.

But the Instructor was confused;
The answer, somehow, held no water —
He could only conclude that East is East of West;
They'd never catch up nor understand
  The new! All new! So very new!

POETRY

SUCCESS STORY FROM AN ECONOMIC ENGINEER

I took my ABC
1 2 3 for advanced aberrendophilia
at M.I.T.
Specializing in
Compressed Expanders, with 4-way pulsifyers
(Dynaforged on the logical principle
That torque was tantamount) and
As for belt-driven universals in cancelling phases
Everything has already gone over to
Rotogenetics; now
Employing the theory of cellular disintegration
I was ready
For a theoretical centrification
Of opposed exemplyfiers -
Whereas
Old B.F. had never taken his M.S. and
Though a good man
Around instantaneous decibles
He'd never really gone beyond
Shock-insulated spacifiers, being willing
To coast among the Suspension People
With their low-hung sibernetics
And latent octograms, thus
When they asked me, had I had
Exploded harmonics with refurberation exemplification
I was able to say Yes
And moved up
From there
Into hypothetical X-23's with perpetuating
Detonations; I was ready, at last
For eradification.

AN UNCONTRIVED OBITUARY

When they ground up my Grandmother
To make into isotypes
For the feeding of the poor-
she became, for the first time, a woman of parts;
But I prefer to remember her as a whole.

As a child of some century several clocks back
She was, at all times, buzzed by hummingbirds;
And as senior flag-bearer for the W.C.T.U. -
Arrogant, misspent, going round amok
Long after her meddler's license had been suspended.
She is to be lovingly remembered as Right's wretch;
She caned young spawners in their Fords
While making the rounds of lover's lanes
To demonstrate the view

For teams of Korean exchange students
Imported here to peer at U.S. folkways,
And Grandmother,
On touchy occasions
Was often dissuaded from triggering stray dogs
With her BB gun
While the neighbors took note.

Annually, she withheld her dime from national defense,
Mailing it elsewhere as her contribution
To the Society of the Prevention of Nuclear Children,
And I see her now, all of a piece
Cloaked in a flakey white skin designed for some body
Thrice her size,
her cigarette legitimatizing her fourth martini's leer,
Feeling in her bones
A child too wise for her years

POETRY

RETROSPECTIONS OF A MAN LEFT OF CENTER

On many a night pump organs
Leaked protestant hymns
While a chairman fingered his nose to suggest singing
The first and last verses
Before we started to stop waiting
For tardy, promised dignitaries
And I, available always
By dialing toll-free numbers
Smelled the tax-deductable franks and beans;
Had memorized some scratched
Patched footage
Of a 1948 Warehouse strike in Ohio
—produced by a professional do-gooder
Provided somebody
Would remember to bring
The projector.

I travelled light those unilluminated years
Burdened only
With a world's problems; moving
Carefully among ants,
Endeavoring to shackle elephants
With legislation
Which got no farther
Than our rented lofts.
I was a letterhead man; a name
Among the few who strode from the crowd.
Started near the bottom after college,
And NYU,
I worked to the top of the page
And finally
As national chairman
Of the Universal Committee
Moved into the center, heading a petition
To save another Negro boy
From another South.

But;
In a lifetime of selfaddressed envelopes
And collection plates and plate dinners
With 28 peas
The total sound
Of all that money
Was the sound of pennies
Falling into the Grand Canyon
On a stormy afternoon.

Yes, then, men
When they passed the fundboxes the hopeful handfuls
Were on hand, and
Handy with their hands
For the handouts
Of instant coffee, day-old doughnuts,
and handling
Frayed extension cords, signing pledges
And clasping each other in
Undiminished hope; these
The exhausted troops
Lonesomely bivouacked somewhere between extinction
And the Third Camp. And I as officer
Whispered strategy
From third-floor quarters; a captain
Until the eviction for five months unpaid rent.

Was it all
Actually
Really worth it? You ask
And I answer with questions; yet
On remembered,
On fewer nights, hot with moon
In some rented park, folk-singers
Exorcised the case
Of mankind's unkindness
To man
With guitars, with banjoes and the
Complaining human falsetto.

POETRY

And sometimes, yes.
Admittedly sometimes something
Right and precious was caught
And held there; clutched
With our fumbling hands
As a new coin from the hardening year.
To this the startled eye, returning asks
What is left
After having been right
By moving to the left
For so long a time?

THE COLD WAR REAFFIRMED

On that occasion
Among occasional occasions
They called it an occasion
And got together
And came apart
Reassuring the world there's no escape
No, on that occasion
There was no place to hide
They said O, no
Place to hide they said no
On that occasion
Among the occasional occasions.

Think of the energy, O the energy
The spent energy of energy spent
As carelessly spent as
Money
The energy
As though it required no energy
To spend energy spent the
Energy spent to spend money.

The world is in a state
The state of the state
Is worldwide as stated
By leading statesmen and the State
Is all it is all states
Laminated
In lamentation
For the state of the state
Is understated.

Then
On that occasional occasion among occasions
They got together to come apart
Resolved that the spent energy spent
to hide the fact there's no place to hide
The fact

POETRY

There exists no place to hide
And announced that the state of the state
Requires the immediate expenditure
Of energy, yes, no they said
Yes no place to hide
The understatement
Of the occasion on the occasion
Of stating the state of the state.

A HIGH ECHELON DISCOURSE

On that last night we turned
Once more to watch
And hear the final explosions
And, I think, a series of imagined cries
Obviously from someone
Who still had tongue
And memory.

O, hell, darling,
The woman said
Clutching, then dropping
A shattered arm
O, hell, it
All seems so unnecessary
And yet
I suppose it was, wasn't it?
Necessary, I mean.

And the General
Placed his unshattered arm around
His effusive daughter
A girl wooed & won by armies all
And with liquid eye
Affixed, still to the miracle
Told us
You've got to fight fire with fire

POETRY

VERNACULAR FOR A GIRL OFF ON A YACHT

Long in Shorts, intimately sunned by inference
Yours was a figure
Of speech.
And to wipe away the shots fired by cold men in heat
You wore my love on your sleeve, Mate,
And when once married,
Twice,
Thrice
you swung wildly at mooring
To chafe other derelicts in the crowded channels
With a yawning, gnawing
Excuse me, sir!
During which time men rowed in tightening circles,
All of them glowing warmly round the equator
After your sun had set.

And I smoked more than most of them drank,
Sleeping less, with considered effort
While you yearned for piracy,
Drifting downstream,
Dragging anchor to some revisited lighthouse,
Or, going into the wind,
Taut-sheeted and trim,
You tacked at angles across the vapor trails
That were left behind by jealous matrons;
Leapt the swells rolled down to you
By men with lonely yens for islands; your bow-wave
Was splendid cleavage for marriage, for divorce;
Your wake-
A helmsman's whistle in the night,
Corkscrewing around,
trailed by sharks,
Good for a round-trip to any of your men.

POETRY

THE ARCH-ANGEL OF MATERIA MEDICA

Miss Flounce, the lab technician
Carries her head on one side, to starboard,
As she tacks toward the chimp cages;
Foul weather's ahead; the ventilators
Have never quite become conditioned
To the cries and sighs, to formaldehyde or urine
And the acrid flavors of panic.
Yet, she insists we're all one happy family here
    (The hamster with electrodes in his eye sockets)
    (The skinned rabbit in the smoke-machine)
    ("Billie" whose brains were homogenized
        By centrifugal force)
    (At a record speed of 9548 r.m.p.s.)

"Nobody," she assures everyone,
"Nobody never, ever had more love and sympathy
For God's poor, dear little creatures."
    (Than the team here at _____Institute.)
Consider "Stumpy"
    Who gave up his legs for the gravity experiment;
Or "Sparks" — the Collie with a radio inside the brain cavity.
Why!
    Fire a pistol beside his ear?
    He wags his tail
    And urinates into his little plastic tube.

Both of them have wonderfully normal appetites.
(Though they'll vomit, naturally,
Into the 10 cc sterilized bags
Attached to the holes in their ribs)
    (Because they're proving the F2 xr 9x32A
    Is directly related to TE 123456)
    (Which, like, is Tennis Elbow —
    Like, you know?)
It looks just like Campbell's Tomato-Beef soup
    When it flows.
    Doesn't it?

POETRY

>Or don't it?

We say a lot of parenthetical things around here.
(That's because so many unasked questions
Have to be answered
Before they're asked.)
Quite understandably the visitor is taken aback
By the gibbon screaming gibberish
As the stretching devices tick off important information.
But wait!
>The transistorized censors
>Know the exact moment the bone will snap
>And will administer the anesthetic accordingly.
Miss Flounce understands the outsider's revulsion:
("I felt the same as you or anybody else
Until I had myself wired for rationalization.")
Similarly, Dr. E.J.E. And the young student from U.S.C.
With the liquid eyes and gentle manners. (Right, Harry?)
He wouldn't harm a fly unless it served some medical experiment.
>(Right, Harry?)

Of course, crusty old Dr. Slicer will say "Let's face it!
We torture animals so people will suffer less."
Yet, every endeavor is made —
Every possible endeavor —
Even impossible endeavors —
>To alleviate suffering —
And Herman Slicer wouldn't be himself
Why! He'd be beside himself
If he didn't make a special trip in the middle of the night
To check up on little Nutsy,
(The squirrel with the chrome helmet
In the concussion chamber.)

A little before noon
(though none of us watch the clock)
All members of the staff begin to salivate.
(Which should tell you a lot
About the psychological state

Of dedicated people who don't mind breaking a leg (ha-ha)
For a sacred purpose.)
Harry can easily handle two Big Macs and a malt
Dr. Slicer will hang up his spotless white coat
And dine at the University Club
With a Mrs. Phonic, whose husband (a strapping young man)
Is presently strapping down gorillas at Cape Canaveral.
Miss Flounce will take her brown bag
And share it with the spoiled, soiled swans
By the creek under the sycamores
If her used car salesman can't make it.
***Pavlov**, the airdale, will doze fitfully*
Through lunch hour, until three;
Then a small explosive planted inside him will detonate,
Announcing feeding time. Usually, he's not hungry:
Nor is the beagle mischieviously named "Flattie Ferguson."
    (You see — there's insufficient space
    Inside his stomach to hold an Aspirin)
    (That's because 5G's of pressure were
    Carefully applied against his ribs.
    He looks like a dog cut out of a shag rug.
    In fact, well, if you try to stand him up
    he tips over)
    (Which, you know? Since he can't exercise
    He doesn't require much food for energy anyhow.)
It is said the Astronauts would've never got far
If it weren't for good old "Flattie Ferguson."

The Rabbit Team?
Though not so dramatic a medical breakthrough —
Or the noble work being done by cockroaches
In the cancer ward
Are testing M'Lady's cosmetics.
Let it be said that a coughing Belgian Hare with running eyes
Would not be first not to be last
To demonstrate that a certain brand of mascara
Implanted in the eyes
Is something to be sneezed at.

POETRY

       (Miss Flounce has vowed not to use _____
       (Manufactured by _____)
  Until Peter's eyes can be reopened)
(parenthetically, she alludes to a cryptic remark
Dropped by an Arab student from N.Y.U.
(No longer affiliated with us)
Who asked, "But isn't this robbing Peter (rabbit)
       To pay Paula?"
(End of parentheses)

A little old lady in Guccis asks
What right have we — to burn off a rabbit's nose
For some Playboy Bunnie's vanity?
And like,
       Would the apes in the Lipstick Experiment
       Return the kiss?
       Will the cocker spaniel
           Whose eyes have been smeared with $9+23$ 1
           Shed a tear for humanity's plight?

       Should the goat with one side of his face removed
           Turn the other cheek?

POETRY

THE PLATINUM PIECE FROM L.A. CAL.

Something from millionaires rubbed off on her
And separated Babe Brown from earth by yachts,
Planes, trains and automobiles with long-hooded power;
Prevented her subsidized ankles from knowing mud
By acts of marble, mink, and parquet floors.
And before her 21st birthday had passed-
    Whoever had, or had had,
    Or had been had, had
  Passed her among their experienced fingers
    Like a hot rivet on Texas oil.

    Babe Brown Weisse De Grot Ferguson Whipple-Lowden
Ortega y Cadiz Warren, with a Shah from E. Persia
    Picked up somewhere along the route
    And discarded in Portugal,
Was glowingly
To be
Polished on and off,
Off and on
By the international varsity; handed on down
To the badminton set,
Stripped of her sapphires, and the able sable plating
Peeled off to disclose the truth
    The wonderous truth
    That the Deity had given everything
      The Deity had to give here; why?

Fertilized and propagated
While champagne was dumped among her thighs
Her hair was crowned a thousand time by dukes, thieves,
    Barons, a Buick dealer,
      Two heavyweight champions
      And a pinball man from Vegas.

In and out of her they came and went like old women
Trying hats for size, till finally,
Like the sun itself, her years cooled; the lovers left.
Each hauling away his quota of guaranteed voltage,

POETRY

And the confounding memory of her steaming lingerie.
And the wives of mistress's lovers looked to
The long-awaited lethargy,
And moved over to make room for one more; the new model,
Longer, lower, and completely automatic.

A LITERARY UNDERGROUND TO THE NORTH: AN ADDENDA

On religious holidays atheistic
Aesthetic, anarchistic
And un-athletic
Young San Francisco
    Disifiliaphiles
Apply their sandals to the throttles
Of massproduced motorcars
    (reactionary old coupes
    With decadent licenseplates
  And inbred chrome)
And journey to democratic Tomales Bay
Deep into the Rexroth country; a windy place
On the left side of the sea.

And here,
While the unmentionables of Bohemian girls are profiled
By the promising stretch of wind-driven yardage
Casually dismantle their trousers
To display —
    Midst tangled kelps, kleenex, milk cartons
    And cormorants slain
    By the vigilant .22's of sons
    of civilservicemen
— Their categorical imperatives.

The shoreline at tide's lowest is high
With the collective gases
Of rotted capitalistic mud; and oysterhusks
Flung there
From the numerous socialist picnics.
And financial octopi,
As resident landlords
Hide inside
Balding automobile tires rolled there
By carefree young revolutionists.
And throughout long, meditiative Sunday evenings
The only sounds are of zealots

POETRY

Belching adamantly among the proletariat;
Or reciting salami
Into the startled ears of Stanford girls
While dialectic materialists
Increase the masses by sleeping
To the left of the body on the right.

THE PHYSICS OF LIGHTER-THAN-AIR OBJECTS, INCLUDING PEOPLE

Wanda, preposterous & serene in bib-overalls
Wears, this morning, her no-nonsense face.
  (A privilege earned
  By the arithmetic
  Of youth subtracted
  From the World's age
  During an odd fraction
  Of U.S. history)

She stares back at the breakfast as though
— Having seen one before —
Our interests should be directed
   To some other topic:
Racoons in general
Or Gravity in particular. Gravity?
It should be a magnetic topic of conversation
On this, a sunwashed morning,
With bees over the honey over the biscuits;
And Yellowjackets flying reconaissance
over bacon and eggs.

"Everything's being sucked toward the ground
By unexplained forces!" She announces accusingly,
And a teaspoon clatters on the bricks,
Ending all argument:
But not the monologue. "Rocks resist —
If they're large enough,
And turtles or alligators and others, wise."
  This is said to mean that animals
  That do everything lying down
  Are able to compensate
  For the energy squandered
  By birds and airplanes,
  Or those extravagant creatures
   That jump or jog.
But gravity, in the end, always wins: That's why

POETRY

We invent schemes of heaven.
"Quite plainly," she says,
(And her face verifies the point)
"We've always envied weightlessness and don't know it."
Excluding those animals
That destroy energy
By Jogging?
Exclusion granted: now, as coffee cools,
And the butter melts,
One is informed that Gravity is Hell —
Always trying to pull us down there,
Always holding fast to everything we'd lift
—Even as we longingly stare at a dandelion
As it glides away.
Heaven, oppositely, in this tug of war,
Would pull us from our shoes and bodies.
So we die; and God, not strong enough
To lift a few pounds,
Settles for weightlessness spirits: like dust,
Or hot-air balloons.

    The summation, be advised, is rather heavy
    For early morning on the desert,
    For a hawk in a holding pattern
    And lizards doing push-ups.
    But I see a small, real cloud against our blue;
    Already weary of arguing with gravity,
    So I know Wanda's game will be rained-out,
    "Go on!" I tell her, "It's all very interesting."

"WANDA" #3

When I first met her — or was I third? —
Wanda was a self-winding clock;
Constantly to be unsprung against time-machines
She converted water and sunlight into the energy of tears
And singlehandedly caused a shortage of yachts
    among recent bachelors of science.

Nowadays, as a readymade biped
She still talks about her fun zone
As though it were some public place
Regularly visited by the underprivileged.
But wait! But nonetheless —
She goes on insisting that old age
    Is a crime
    Punishable by death.

Granted: her heart belongs to her father's
               only daughter.
And sex is an item she has indexed and placed
In the filing cabinet with other misbegotten investments.
So, tell her of Darwin's theories; suddenly erect,
She yawns in anticipation,
But is interrupted by her hair
Which blows up an appointment in 27 seconds
Though she shall never live to know
    How late it is.

POETRY

"WANDA" #4

Around sundown
All the world's tides move beggingly toward us.
We slant away from each other in aluminum chairs
Searching deep to perplexities
As though fixed stares
Can expose truths for the challenging.

Across our valley
Animals friendly or enemy
Threaten each other good night; imitating us
With official bravado
    Or feigned innocence.
Stealthily a breeze has crossed us with sycamore trees.
A cold shadow passes her forehead,
And her thigh sends me the last heat of twilight.
Now the surf holds back for seven beats.
So we listen for the sound of each other's hearts —
Neither of us certain whose has stopped: legally,
Wanda is still alive
And clears her throat for proof.

I, on cue, say "Schopenhauer's watching us again!"
For who else sits the third chair
Impatiently timing our delusion on his minute-hand
While her east eyebrow climbs toward the first star?

"WANDA" #5

"Love forces you to become more honest
And tell more lies," Wanda says truthfully, and,
Softened eyes lowered
To fly at half mast
She decides that God's first mistake
        was dividing the molecule
So that forever, and a day later,
Everyone must go around searching for his other half.
    A head dips abruptly:
    Long, lacquered hair salutes profundity:
    The thought marches rigidly onward:
"And not finding it, men had to invent boats or cars
And Veal Scallopini, guns, business."
        A glance from her lowering, faulted left eye
        Completes the sentence.
        But I've lost the subject;
        The eyelid hangs in there,
        Threatening love —
        Were there presently a man worthy of fighting —
And it also warns of men to come — long lines
Of grasping Pilgrims
Ready to bare their own violence. So,
I shift my attention to things less competitive —
A sycamore tree with dying branches serves me well
Because in it, suddenly important,
Is last summer's bird nest.
Love flew away —
Leaving only sexless chirps and broken shells
And an urge to scratch out insects
Until such time Darwin might
        Blow his whistle again

We, please understand,
Are unable to transcend constant glands;
We wait to pounce at ungiven times
For an ecstasy of low moans and arched necks
And a celebration of the death of honor.

POETRY

"WANDA" #7

"There's nothing so ignoble
As a small, bald, rotund old man
Leaving the door of a prostitute's flat
Unless he happens to be
Igor Stravinsky."
      I think of Wanda making time go away
      With observations like this
      As she dabs unlighted cigarettes
      Into ashtrays no longer there.

When surrounded by parties of the first choice
She lets her tan, smooth thighs go public, then,
Leaning forward to breast group awe —
While a curious silence passes unnoticed —
She'll reassure everyone that she didn't make it up
For the patent expired long since;
      And I don't mind —
      It enables her to withhold her hidden assets.

I do feel sorry for hairless men, and short,
Especially if they're fat and thin,
And unable to get away until their alarms ring.
But I am also banking some sadness for Wanda
With an inordinately high rate of interest
When men no longer leave her walk-up flat.

POETRY

IN THE CITY, IN THE CITY

The sky, this curious morning
Has been flown in from some other time or place.
It leers blue and innocent of stings and acids.
But malingering here sans passport or tourist visa,
It glances 'round nervously,
Poised tense, like migrating ducks
On some unfamiliar pond
Quite aware it should quickly move on
Before trouble.

We gaze upwards, pleased but alarmed,
Vaguely recognizing some forgotten heritage
With escalating resentment
Because this unauthorized purity dirties us all the more.
Understandably then,
Our sex is cocked by transparent strangers
Who hurry past with pre-recorded apologies.
An addict who hasn't made a try for days
Suddenly steps out and asks:
And there is knowing in the eyes.
A hibernating taxi thaws in the new, odd sun
Then trumpets war
'Gainst a stalled, urinating bus.
And we, moving in righteous anger
Over broken telephone connections
Fire profane volleys
At a drunk raised from the gutter by weird illumination
While cops jostle
Only to dream of outboard motorboats
*   On newly recalled bays.*

It is a time to impeach a mayor
Or bomb the subways
Or inaugurate a new series of brownstone burglaries
Or fire a gun; for children to experience
Their seasonal rape;
For another tenement couple —

POETRY

> *Having hoarded years all their lives —*
> *To resent the sky*
> *And begin once more to move away.*

Corrupt politicians might consider
Turning themselves in on such a day;
Well-dressed, muttering men will discover
They've nothing to shout at the psychologically deaf.
We glimpse our pull-down mouths on cracked windows
And blame it all on the weather;
> Why isn't it like this every day?

APPENDIX

APPENDIX

A Curtis Zahn Resume (1956-1987)

I) PLAYS, PRODUCED AND/OR PUBLISHED

(1) Curtis Zahn has been a playwright-in-residence at:

Academy Theater, Atlanta, GA.
Barter Theatre, Abingdon, W. Va.
Edward Ludlum Theater, Los Angeles, Ca.
White Barn Theatre, Conn.

(2) Playscripts published in:

Broadway Plays, Inc., N.Y.
Experiment Magazine, Wash.
First Stage Magazine, Purdue University
Poetry & Drama Magazine, N.Y.
West Coast Plays, San Francisco, Ca.

(3) Productions and Scripts:

An Albino Kind of Logic
Academy Theater, Atlanta
Il Caffe Magazine, Italy (published)
Catawba College, Salisbury, N.C.
Century Playhouse, Los Angeles
Edward Ludlum Theater, Los Angeles
First Stage Magazine (published)
Globe Theater, San Diego, Ca.
Hudson College, N.Y.
Oxford Theater, Los Angeles
Pacifica Players, Los Angeles
Radio Illinois
Rising Sun Theater, N.Y.C.
San Diego Jewish Center, Ca.
San Diego State College
University of Buffalo, N.Y.
White Barn Theatre, Conn.

Conditioned Reflex

Academy Theater, Atlanta
Actors Studio West, Los Angeles
Barter Theater, Abingdon, W. Va.
Edward Ludlum Theater, Los Angeles
First Stage Magazine (published)
Pacifica Radio, Los Angeles, Berkeley, N.Y.C.
Positano Coffeehouse, Malibu, Ca.
Theatre De Lys, N.Y.C.
White Barn Theatre, Conn.

Confrontation
Actors Studio West, Los Angeles
Berghoff/Hagen Workshop, N.Y.C. (reading)
New Playwrights Theater, Los Angeles

Five, Four, Three, Two, One
Barnsdall Theater, Los Angeles
Pilot Theater, Los Angeles
Poetry & Drama Magazine (published)
Theater-of-Note, Los Angeles
U.N. Players, Donnelly Library Theater, N.Y.C.

Genesis & Exodus of Operation X
Theatre Vangard, Beverly Hills, Ca. (reading)

In a Name, Nothing
Experiment Magazine Anthology, Wash. (published)

Landscape with Figures
Theatre Rapport, Los Angeles

Origin of the Species
Theater-of-Note, Los Angeles

Purgation & Re-entry of Group 89
Pan Andreas Theater, West Hollywood, Ca. (staged reading)

Reactivated Man
Broadway Plays, Inc. (published)
Edward Ludlum Theater, Los Angeles
Johathon Cape, Ltd., London (published)

Los Angeles County Anti-Nuclear Festival
New Directions, N.Y.C. (published)
Pacifica Radio, Berkeley
Penguin Books, England (published)
Suhrkampff Verlag, W. Germany (published)
West Coast Plays, San Francisco (published)

Sadco
Ash Grove Coffeehouse, Los Angeles
Cinema Theatre, Los Angeles
Claremont Colleges Arts Festival (reading)
Coronet Theater, Los Angeles
First Stage Magazine (published)
First Unitarian Church, Los Angeles
Radio Berliner, W. Germany
Santa Monica Playhouse, Santa Monica, Ca.
Venice Pavillion, Los Angeles

Secretly Disarmed
The Rookery, Costa Mesa, Ca.
Theater-of-Note, Los Angeles

Under-Ground
Angry Arts Festival, Los Angeles
Edward Ludlum Theater, Los Angeles
First Stage Magazine (published)
Pilot Theater, Los Angeles
White Barn Theatre, Conn.

II) FICTION

(1) Book: *American Contemporary.* New York, San Francisco: New Directions/San Francisco Review; Suhrkampff Verlag, W. Germany; Jonathon Cape, Ltd., England; Penguin Books, England; 1963. (Short story collection.)

(2) Short stories published in:
Abyss
Artesian

Bard Review
Best American Short Stories
Breakthru
Il Caffe (Italy)
Coastlines
The Colorado Review
Contemporary Fiction
Contour
El Corno Emplumando (Mexico)
Daily World
Decades of Short Stories
Doubt Magazine
Emergent
Exile Press
Fanfare
Fascination
First Person
The Folio
Grotesste Review (England)
Helena Brecht-Weill Monologue Troupe (Germany)
Idiom
The Kapustkan
Liberation
The Light Year
Literary Artpress
Literary Messenger
Magazine San Diego
Mica
Miscellaneous Man
Monocle
Neon
New Mexico Quarterly
New West
Nimrod
Olivant Quarterly
Outcry (New Zealand)
Outdoors
Prairie Schooner

Quixote (Spain)
Real Romances
The Roadrunner
San Francisco Review
Script
Sir
Sketch
Southern Literary Messenger
Symbolica
Trails
Venture
Westscribe
The Window (England)
Wormwood Review (England)
Write

(3) Stores have appeared in anthologies published via:
Angler's Choice
Anti-Story
Ill Caffe (Italy)
Change Over
Cross Section
Jonathon Cape, Ltd. (England)
Librarie Terminales (France)
Manifesto
New Directions
Penguin Books (England)
Prison Etiquette
Quixote (Spain)
Suhrkampff Verlag (W. Germany)

III) POETRY

(1) Poetry has appeared in these journals:
American Muse
American Poetry
Approach
Artesian

Ball State Forum
Beecher's Press
Berkeley Review
Beyond Baroque
Black Cat
The Bridge
Il Caffe (Italy)
California Quarterly
Cal State Quarterly
Circle
City Lights
Clarte' (Sweden)
Climax
Coastlines
Coercion
Combustion
Contact
El Corno Emplumando (Mexico)
Deer & Dachshund
Different View
East & West
Electrum
Epos
Etcetera
Existaria
Fellowship
Fiddlehead (England)
First Person
Four Winds
Frontier
Gale
Galley Sail
Goosetree Press
Grotesste Review (England)
Half Moon
Henny Penny
Houynenyms (Australia)
Inferno

Inscape
Kaleidoscope
Kapustkan
Letter Among Friends
Liberation
Light Year
Literary Artpress
Mainstream
Matrix
Mendicant
Merlin's Magic
Midwest Review
Miscellaneous Man
Morning Star
Mutiny
Neo
New Poets
New West
New Yorker
Nomad
Odyssey
Old Palace (England)
Outcry
The Outsider
Parnassus
Poetry Hour
Poetry, Los Angeles
Quicksilver
Renaissance
San Francisco Review
Sciamachy
Snowy Egret
South & West
Southwest Review
Span
Sun
Symbolica
Targets

Trace
21st Century (Australia)
U.S. Poetry
View
Views
Wanderlust
Whetstone
Wormwood Review
Xanadu
Yellow Silk

(2) Poetry has appeared in these anthologies:
American College Poetry
The American Muse
American Poetry
A Canadian Anthology
El Corno Emplumando (Mexico)
Crazy Horse (Tom McGrath, Editor)
Experimental Theatre Anthology
In-Sert
Live Poetry (Kathleen Koppel, Editor)
Long Beach University Press
Mainstream Anthology
New Orlando Poetry
New Poets
The Nonexistent City, Coastlines Press
Pata Rocni Doba (Czech., Walter Lowenfels, Editor)
Poetry and Drama (Alan Swallow, Editor)
Poetry, Los Angeles
Poets of Today (Walter Lowenfels, Editor)
Seeds of Liberation (Paul Goodman, Editor)
Trace (James Boyer May, Editor)
Treasures of Parnassus
Xanadu Annual

(3) Poetry Readings and Performances
Algonquin West Readings
Artists for Survival / Target L.A.
Beverly Hills Bicentennial Poetry

Beyond Baroque
Claremont Colleges Literary Arts Festival
Jazz Meets Poetry (Cosmo Alley Coffeehouse, L.A.)
Laguna Poets Series
Los Angeles Museum of Science Series
Orange County Poets / Irvine College
Poetry Los Angeles Series
Poets' Gathering
Positano Coffeehouse, Malibu, Ca
Pacifica Radio / tapes
Unitarian Festival of the Arts
United Nations Players / verse drama
University of Southern California
Upstart Crow / Rookery Readings
Zahn Street / Xoregos Dance Company, with voices

IV) BIOGRAPHICAL SOURCES

(1) *Various*
American Literary Guild
Boston University / Curtis Zahn Collection
Coda
Contemporary Authors
Dictionary of International Biography
Dramatists Guild Quarterly
Encyclopedia of Short Fiction (Virginia Commonwealth University)
Eugene Field Society
Genesis West / interview
Lincoln Center / Performing Arts Library, N.Y.C. / Curtis Zahn Collection
National Playwrights Directory
"On Writers" (Series: Los Angeles Times)
Plays & Playwrights
Plays & Playwrights Index
Trace / Invitation to Reading
Who's Who in the West
Writer's Who's Who

197

(2) *Awards*
   Dylan Thomas Poetry Award
   Golden Globe Award, Globe Theatre, San Diego (six awards for production of *An Albino Kind of Logic)*

V) EDITORIAL AFFILIATIONS

(1) *Editor, Co-Editor*
   Coastlines Magazine: Editor, antiwar issue
   Roadrunner Magazine: Co-editor
   Westscribe Magazine: Co-editor
   Yachting Annual (San Diego): Editor/Publisher

(2) *Associate Editor*
   Compass Magazine
   Coronado Citizen
   Trace Magazine

VI) WORK IN PROGRESS

(1) Fiction:

   The Absolutely Naked Truth About My Problem: In this volume; is part of a longer work in progress.
   Decentralia, Minor (Novel)
   28 Collected Stories

(2) Drama:

   Americana 3000 A.D.: In progress.
   The Escape, Purgation, and Re-entry of Group N-17: Recently completed; unproduced.
   Genesis and Exodus of Operation X + Zero
   In a Name, Nothing: In progress (rewrite).
   The Plight of the Lesser Sawyer's Cricket: Recently completed; unproduced.
   Respectfully Yours . . . . : In progress (rewrite).
   The Transistorized Butter Knife

(3) Poetry:

*Standing Aghast in the Present Tense Imperfect
(collected poetry)*